About the Author

When I was 11 my cat died. When I was 12, my grandfather died. When I was 13 my father died. After that, we were always having to move house. There were five of us, four sisters and a brother. I was the second eldest. Our mother wrote children's stories to support us and I typed them out. I left school at 16 and worked as a journalist.

What I most wanted to do was to live in a little cottage in the woods and grow strawberries and gooseberries. These days I do, and it's a bit like where Miss Ada and Miss Lily live in Pegg Bottom. Like them, I have to chop fuel for the fires and there are mice up in the roof. Unlike them, I have a husband, four grown-up children, and a grandson.

Rachel Anderson

Blackthorn, Whitethorn

Rachel Anderson

Hodder Children's Books

a division of Hodder Headline plc

Typeset by Avon Dataset Ltd, Bidford-on-Avon, Warks

Printed and bound in Great Britain by
Mackays, Chatham, Kent

Hodder Children's Books
A division of Hodder Headline PLC
338 Euston Road
London NW1 3BH

Contents

for Ann Hynes

ONE

When it was summer

My first notebook begins here

Such pleasant family life

Roundabout the middle of last holidays, something very, very and really truly mega-death dreadful began to happen to me, and to Esther and to our Mum who is quite nice really and deserved better. In fact, to the whole family. Even Mrs Tiggywinkle was affected by it, she perhaps the worst of all. It was so dreadful that for quite a long while it's been making me sick even thinking about it.

It was started by our Dad. He did a dastardly deed that he shouldn't have done, something he could have gone to prison for. In the olden days, they sent them to the debtors' goal. Even this century there was a man who did a dodgy banking deal in Singapore and they've only just let him out, seven long years later. When he first got locked up, he was quite dishy. Or so Esther says because she can remember back that far. Now he looks wasted.

'Don't know why his girlfriend stuck by him,' Esther said. 'Sure *I* wouldn't.'

I can't bear to imagine what our Dad would look like after seven years in an Asian cell. He's gone gaunt and grey just in the past few weeks living here.

Luckily, our Dad didn't get sent to prison, even though his business partner, or rather, ex-business partner, did. As the judge at the trial said, 'Ultimately, the only person you have seriously damaged in your incompetent dealings, is yourself. And that is a hurt you will have to live with for a long time.'

The judge was wrong. If you're a grown man and you hurt yourself, you also hurt your wife and your children.

'Your poor innocent and *defenceless* children!' said Esther. She's been leaning over my shoulder, reading every word I'm writing. 'Put that in, Hannah. "Defenceless". That's what we are. Pile on the pathos, in case he ever reads it.'

'For goodness sake, Ess,' I snapped. 'This isn't meant for *him* to read. Or anybody else. It's personal. It's for *me*.'

'What a selfish brat you are. Don't you want to share your words of wisdom which chronicle our family's time of suffering?'

I ignored her. I went on writing.

So, if you're a businessman who hurts himself, you also hurt your most beloved younger daughter's cat, Mrs Tiggywinkle. And your elder daughter's guinea pig (not that Esther seemed too bothered when her guinea pig keeled over). Unintentionally or not, Dad hurt us so much that it made me be copiously sick all over his incredible big car with the white leather seats and the air-conditioning and the brilliant sound system with the four speakers so you felt you were in the Albert Hall. That was just before the bailiffs came to take it away. Dad knew they were on their way so he took us for one last spin.

Whatever Esther says, I'm not totally defenceless. As time passes, I'm beginning to be able to set it all down in order to try to get it out of my system.

'In order to purge yourself,' Esther corrected me.

'What?' I said.

'You are writing it down for the purgative and carthatic effect. To make you sick. To get rid of it.'

'Ssh,' I said. *I'm* meant to be the one who's writing a chronicle. Not her. But being twenty-three and a half months older, she always thinks she knows more about everything.

I said, 'And will you please stop craning round my neck and reading over my shoulder. I'm beginning to find it irritating.'

'Oh very well then, Miss Hoity-Toity,' she said and she skipped out of the bedroom leaving the door wide open which left me in a draught so I've had to get up and close it and put on another pair of thick socks (hers) before I die of hypothermia.

Feeling cold all the time is another of the things that is definitely our Dad's fault, a direct result of the money muddle he got himself into.

Our Dad's troubles started to break loose in the second week of the holidays. A Thursday, and sunny. Funny how you remember small, unimportant details. It was afternoon. It began with the phone ringing, not that it seemed significant at the time. The telephone rings often enough. That's what they're for.

Bleep bleep bleep. Drat! there's that phone again. Who can it be this time?

I hardly even took it in. I knew it wouldn't be for me. It never was. It was either for Mum from one of her friends about the Neighbourhood Watch meeting, or a bridge party, or a charity fashion show. Or else one of Esther's pals networking. Another superb outing to ten-pin bowling, or swimming club, or aerobics, or to wander round the Mall boy-watching. In fact, I guessed that's what it must be because of the way, even though Esther was pretending to be asleep, she responded to the beeping tone.

She'd been lying out on the lounger on the new patio getting her legs brown, ready for when we went off to the villa Dad rents us in Tenerife. (I warned her that sun-bathing's bad for your health.)

'Drat!' she said. 'I knew I should've brought Mum's mobile out.'

She got up to answer it indoors, ambling in, leggy and languid. Just occasionally, I can see why the boys fancy her.

I thought, Tenerife = nightmare.

The local lads'll be ogling round the villa like flies. I'll have to elbow them out of the way just to get down the steps and across the beach to the sea.

That phone-tone whining away through the house signalled

the day when all previous life, as we Broddys (not forgetting Mrs Tiggywinkle and Esther's guinea-pig, now deceased) knew it, was about to end.

Broddys' Bad New Year

So it's September. We're now into the second month of the Broddys' All-Change Year and it's turning out to be stranger and mostly more horrible than any other year I, or anybody else, has ever lived.

As any person who has ever been given an electronic personal organiser, with its amazingly far-sighted calendar stretching right up to 2099 (or any person who's been given one of those five-year manually-lockable diaries) knows, all normal years begin on 1st January.

If you're still young, the year begins after you've been sent to bed so you don't even notice it. You say goodnight to your parents who are in their festive finery, Dad in his black silky evening suit, Mum in her shimmery midnight blue taffetta evening gown. Dad cracks a joke. Instead of, 'Nighty-night! See you in the morning,' he says, 'Nighty-night! See you *next year*!'

You giggle, then up to bed, fall asleep, and sure enough, when you wake, you find it really *is* the next year, though if you go alone to your sister's room and say to her how strange it is that it doesn't feel any different from yesterday, she throws a pillow at your head and says, 'You silly duffer! Of course it's next year! Can't you feel it in your soul? Don't you understand *anything?*'

When you're a bit older, like I was *last* 31st December, you're allowed to sit up with Esther and the student from further along Buccleigh Gardens who was our sort of person-sitter.

'The hired slave,' Esther called her, even to her face. Esther had this dream that when our Dad got really rich, she'd have someone like Virginia for her personal maid. 'To do my bidding. How much an hour are you paying her, Dad?'

Back in those days, before the troubles, our parents were always prancing off to parties and dances and mayor's receptions. They used to call up a chauffeured hire-car to take them, to save the bother of having to drive themselves.

These days we haven't even got a phone, let alone four wheels.

So there we were at the end of last year, Esther and I and the student called Virginia, staying up late, watching telly, eating pop-corn and setting fire to raisins in brandy snitched from Dad's drinks cabinet. We sat through all the variety programmes till the moment new year actually happened. Then, on the first stroke of midnight, we did daft things that Virginia taught us, like jumping off the back of the new sofa Dad gave Mum for Christmas.

'Why?' I squealed. 'Why are we doing this?'

'Just do it!' said Esther. 'Because O'Gradey says!'

'It's to make sure we all get plenty of smashing good luck in the coming year,' Virginia explained. Next, she told us we had to race round the outside of the house, in our pyjamas and dressing-gowns, to make absolutely certain that the good luck we'd conjured up by jumping off the back of the sofa, stayed with us.

That was our babysitter's belief. And because she was at sixth-form college taking A-levels, we believed her. What a load of poppycock. Not one tiny bit of luck stayed inside. It all seeped out of the French windows and under the door and away down Buccleigh Gardens. It makes me feel sick again, just remembering. But I *have* to remember so I can set it down.

Esther, who is once again reading over my shoulder because she is incredibly nosey, pointed out that I am making false assumptions about new years.

'Really, Han! You're so narrow-minded. And ignorant. For instance, what about Chinese New Year? That happens in February and it doesn't have a number but the name of an animal. Right now we're in the year of the rabbit or the rooster or some farmyard thing.'

'Most likely the year of the skunk,' I snarled. 'Because that's what it definitely feels like, specially with *you* in it.'

Esther's been bored all day, just itching to pick a fight with me.

That phone call, back in the last school holidays, which marked the change in our lives.

Esther slouched sullenly back to the patio to finish toasting her shins. 'Wasn't for me. For Dad. Something to do with work.'

'You'll give yourself melanomas if you get sun-burned,' I said. 'And then you'll *die*! And I'll be dancing at your funeral.'

She slapped some more oil on.

Dad didn't normally receive work-calls at home. We should have realised it was odd. As it turned out, it was about his non-work. He no longer had any work.

'Sounds like his firm's going to go bust,' said Esther. That didn't explain much to me, though the look on Mum's face did, when she got in. It was as though, on that nice sunny day, Mum had just seen six ghosts all at once, then an aeroplane had dropped on her head.

'Chin up, Mum,' I said. 'Nothing's as bad as all that.' How could it be when we were flying off to the villa next week?

But it seemed it was.

'Broddy Brothers is going into receivership,' Mum said in a flat voice. Note the 'is going.' Not 'are going.'

'What d'you mean?'

Esther cheerfully explained. 'He's borrowed more money than he can afford and he hasn't had time to make it up, and now the people he borrowed from have said it's time to cut their losses.'

'But why would he need to *borrow* money? He's always loaded.'

Esther gave me a withering look. 'Not him personally, you clown. For his business.'

Mum said in a voice as low as a dead man's whisper, 'I think we're going to be repossessed.'

I said, 'Hey! That sounds rude!' I thought being possessed was either something devils did, or wicked men to young maidens.

Esther gave me another of her lemon-juice looks. She always has an advantage over me. I never seem to catch up.

'Repossession means the house is going to be taken away from us.'

'Bit tricky,' I said. 'You can't take a house away, unless it's on wheels. But you'd never manage to fix wheels on a place this size, would you?' Our house in Buccleigh Gardens had a basement half-below ground level. 'Now, if we lived in a caravan, or garden shed, which could be picked up by a crane, it'd be easy for them.'

I thought it was all quite a laugh. That's before I realised it was going to affect me personally. I mean, the school holidays can be quite a draggy time, specially with my friend Katy away so I couldn't go round and play tennis with her. Not being interested in boys with the same fervour as Esther, there wasn't a lot to do.

Esther said, 'They're not going to move the house. It's *us* that has to move. Move out. Then the bank can sell it and realise some of the assets.'

'Whassat?'

How come she knows all these words?

'Get back some of the loot they're owed.'

I said, 'But we've always lived here!' Nearly always. Definitely since I was small. 'Still, a change is as good as a rest. I'd quite like to live where Katy does.' My friend Katy lived at the end of Buccleigh Gardens in a huge house with her own en suite bathroom and a double garage, and an enormous garden with a tennis court that you'd hardly expect to find in a town. Her Dad's a bank manager. It may even be him who lent the money to my Dad.

High finance, low spirits

The weeks leading up to Dad's case were weird and uncertain.

Nobody explained anything. Life seemed to be chugging on nearly as normal. Yet I sensed something wasn't right. It was like a distant itch on somebody else's back, and the phone seemed to be going all the time, even late at night. Dad was coming in and going out at all hours.

'The court's agreed to a month's grace,' I heard Mum telling someone on the phone.

Whatever that meant. Then she was saying how he'd had a massive get-out clause. But that didn't help me either.

Men in stiff, double-breasted suits, with bulging briefcases, kept coming to the house and staying in the dining-room all day. And even Mum, who wasn't supposed to be involved in Broddy Brothers, had to go in and discuss things with them. She always kept a brave face on.

Broddy Brothers was Dad's business. He didn't actually have a brother. Esther says it was called that to make it seem bigger than it was.

Once, I caught Mum sniffing into her hanky behind the freezer in the garage. And Esther took to eavesdropping on all incoming phone-calls. She called it monitoring the situation.

Then suddenly one morning, *wham blam*! there's photographers hanging about in the front drive, and trampling on the flower-beds. And there's journalists ringing on the neighbours' doorbell, trying to get a quote about what kind of scoundrel Dad is. But how would *they* know? Commander and Mrs Jones lived behind their laurel defences and saw our Dad even less than we did.

The photographers got some shots of Dad with his lawyer hurrying out of the house on their way to the Inns of Court for the hearing, and some other ones (which they never used) of Esther leaning provocatively out of her bedroom window. Then they went away to search out some other economic failure to pester.

A person who is declared a bankrupt, which is what our Dad was, has to have their estate administered and disposed of for the benefit of the creditors. 'Estate' doesn't necessarily mean a historic stately mansion in the country with fields and horses and stables. It can just as well mean our comfortable home in Buccleigh Gardens, plus our computers, our furniture, and carpets, and Mum and Dad's cars. If you're a bankrupt you have to be stripped of all your property. (A judge says so.) It sounds old-fashioned and horribly cruel.

It is.

Esther and I may not agree on much. But we both agree that repossession and disposal of estate means the end of one kind of existence which is so nice that you don't even think about it, and the beginning of another nasty one.

Esther has come back into the draughty bedroom. She's leaned over my shoulder again, joggling my arm, and told me that I'd spelled bankrupt wrong.

'There's a *K* in it, you duffer, not a *C*,' she said.

The reason I can't spell properly any more is because the brilliant computer I used to use, which did my spelling for me and which I thought was mine, actually belonged to stupid Broddy Bros. If only I'd known that I only had that spell-check on borrowed time I might have appreciated it more.

'I'll spell it any way I want,' I glowered at Esther. 'So when will you shut shut shut up?'

One of the little-known facts about bankruptcy is that, as a direct result of it, sisters often come to loathe each other out of all proportion to their actual defects.

Belle Vue, Pegg Bottom

Our new address is the worst thing that has happened to me in my whole life. I don't even want Katy to write to me because then she'll find out. The result of Dad's troubles is that we have come to live in a cramped ugly bungalow, with a rusty corrugated tin roof, which is surrounded by a belle vue of stinging nettles, and is situated down the end of a long lane, miles from anywhere. In the hamlet of Pegg Bottom, there are three other dwellings, all abandoned. One even has a baby tree growing out of its chimney.

This seems to be the way Dad wants it.

'To bury his shame from the world's cruel gaze,' says Esther. 'Put that in, Han. It's rather good.'

And Mum tries her best to carry on.

It isn't just losing the house and cars and stuff. It's losing the knowledge that we're a safe contented family. Because we're not.

Esther has taken it into her head to harp on about me writing about how the new year begins on January 1st. She's like a dog with a bone.

'There are in fact, Hannah, my little duckie pet angel, many, many types of new year, quite aside from the calendar year. There is the school year which begins in September. And the university year which begins in October. There is the tax year which begins on April 6th.'

'I wish you'd bog off and leave me alone,' I said. I moved my arm to try to cover the whole page. I smudged the ink in the process. But at least that had the effect of making my sentences illegible. From now on, I'll either have to write in code or find a new hiding place.

In this bad new year which, I insist, began in August, Esther and I have to share a tiny poky bedroom. We've got a pair of clanking metal bedsteads that are so close, they're almost touching. We never used to have to share. We never used to argue. At least, I can't remember that we did. Not as much as this anyhow. It's really evil. But then so are most things.

I said, not calmly, but loudly, 'The starting point for the new school year and the new tax year are both pre-determined. So everybody *knows* when they're going to happen. What *I'm* writing about is a different kind of time which begins without any *pre-announcement*. Suddenly. Unexpectedly.'

There was a clatter at the kitchen door. Mum came in with two casserole dishes, thirteen coat hangers and a telephone, only unfortunately, there's no socket to plug it into. The unpacking process sees to take forever.

'Now then, girls,' she called. The bungalow walls are thin. You hear everything. 'What are you two bickering about now? Can't you come and lend a hand? I thought you might at least have got the tea started. I can't see to everything myself.'

Dad was around somewhere. Probably in bed with his head under the blanket. But the way things are, Mum would never dream of asking *him* to lend a hand.

'We're not bickering, Mum,' I said sweetly. 'Just discussing finance.' I made a vomit face at Esther which Mum didn't see. 'My kind big sister is explaining to me how the start of the tax year is calculated.'

'The *tax* year?' Mum echoed, then sat down at the kitchen table (which is actually a wobbly folding campers' table), put her head in one of the casseroles and began to sob in a restrained way.

These days, it's terribly unsettling talking to her. You never know what word is going to set her off.

Esther and I got the tea. It's always the same. Potatoes and cabbage and, once a week, really nasty cheap mince that's mostly fat.

Esther peeled the potatoes. I chopped the cabbage. Out here in the barren wasteland known as countryside, there are an awful lot of potatoes. They're very cheap. Mum buys them straight from beside the field in a big brown sack. They're encrusted with sandy mud. We always have to have them boiled. Baked would be a thrilling change. But the oven part of the cooker doesn't work. Nobody dares ask Dad to have a look at it.

In our previous existence, we used to have delicious junk food. I'd do anything to be able to dial a number on the phone, put in my order and have a mouth-wateringly scrummy Four Seasons pizza, dripping with melted mozarella, studded with shiny black olives, delivered ten minutes later by a boy on a motor scooter.

I wish I hadn't written that last bit.

Esther must have found out where I've been hiding my notebook (under the mattress). She reads it when I'm not looking. Just as we were going to bed, she said very nonchalantly, 'If ever we get to have a pizza delivery out here, you can stick with the Four Seasons. I'll just have the boy.'

She's right. The worst thing about the countryside isn't that it's wet, cold, dull and full of nothing but sugar beet and potatoes. It's that it's lonely.

Over the weekend, Dad cheered up a bit and helped Mum unpack half a boxful of her books. But it only lasted till Monday morning when it was once again time for him not to be going to work. Then he sank back into gloom.

TWO

Spectres in September

Two sisters

My last notebook's full. And the five-year journal, with real
leather cover and dainty gilt padlock which Dad gave me for
my birthday years ago when I was too young to appreciate
the importance of writing things up, is still missing. I'm really
annoyed. I wanted to use it to continue this important family
chronicle of our sad times. Instead, I'm having to use pages
snipped from the back of an old biology exercise book. I'll
staple them together into a home-made notebook if I ever
find my stapler again.

We're still living out of a muddle of boxes. It's impossible.
They were packed in that traumatic rush. And now Mum's
given up on the unpacking. Perhaps that means we won't be
staying here much longer? Even when I *have* found whatever
I'm looking for, there's nowhere to put it, except the tall creaky
wardrobe in our bedroom. It hasn't got any shelves, the door
swings open all by itself in the dead of night. Anyway, Esther's
put most of her stuff in there already.

I need a nice new notebook, lined, with smooth pages, hard covers, and a combination lock to keep out snoopers. But there's no way I'll get any kind of notebook round here.

At Pegg Bottom, there are no shops, no pavements, no street lights, no phone box, no flipping nothing, just the three tumbledown cottages which look as though they're sinking slowly back into the ground like old mushrooms. But when Esther complained that it's like being banished to live in the bum of beyond, Mum just said, 'Nonsense! A lot of people would give their eye-teeth to be in such a wonderful environment. Away from the hurly-burly where we can breathe properly.'

'Hm,' said Esther. 'Not so sure about Dad's breathing. Looks like he may have died.'

Dad didn't flinch, just sank his unshaven chin further down on his chest and sighed.

Mum glanced at Esther and mouthed, 'Sssh. Don't tease him.'

He's gone practically comatose lately. Sits all day on a broken sun-lounger (one of the bits of Buccleigh Gardens furniture which the bailiffs didn't seem to want to take) staring into Belle Vue's nettle jungle.

Mum says the reason the hamlet's deserted is because there's no more manual jobs in agriculture. 'I dare say this was a busy corner of the world, in the good old days. Still, we'll try our best to make it *our* busy corner, won't we, girls?'

'How?' said Esther. 'We're refugees, displaced persons. You know we don't belong here.'

'No, indeed you don't,' said Mum, pushing us out through the kitchen door. 'Hurry along now or you'll miss that bus again.'

It's a mile and a half up to the cross-roads. That's the nearest place the school coach stops. We walk. Which is quite interesting if you're looking for corpses.

So far, I've found three squashed toads which I offered to Esther to kiss because I thought they were frogs, a bird's skeleton all dry and white dangling in a bush, and a nearly dead hedgehog which Esther told me not to pick up because it was jumping with fleas.

No one else gets on at Hungry Hill. There's just a barn full of potatoes with the wind whistling through its rafters, and another building, all boarded-up. In front of it, there's a post with a wooden cross-piece at the top. It looks to me like a gallows.

'Spooky-scary,' I said. 'To think of the criminals back in Mum's good old days, getting this view as the last thing they saw before they died.'

You can see for miles, across bleak fields and bumpy woods, not quite as far as Pegg Bottom. That's hidden in a dip.

'Crimms?' said Esther. 'Dying? What you on about now?'

'Being executed on that thing.'

'That's not a gallows for *hanging* people, you twerp! Honestly, Han. Sometimes I think your imagination works overtime. It's a post for putting a sign on.'

'Sign?'

'For the name of the pub. Look, it's an old pub. *The Three Magpies*.'

She was right. I saw faded lettering on the walls. 'Oh,' I said, so relieved I felt dizzy. 'I suppose it got closed down when all the people left the land, like Mum says they did.'

Lowly school days

If you missed the school coach, as Esther and I did for the first couple of days because we hadn't estimated just how long a long lane can be, or how many small dead creatures there might be to look at on the way, you had another three-mile trudge to town.

It's called the North County High School. Esther's a bit of a snob and she says it should be called the low school because it's so low in amenities. No library. No swimming pool. No squash courts. No practice studios. (Though actually I'm glad the bailiffs took the viola. I was never going to be any good on it, not even if I practised my arpeggios for a million years.)

The other pupils are low in ambition and competitive spirit. You should see how they play team games, as though they don't really mind which side wins.

None of the teachers seemed bothered when we turned up late on our first morning. We'd walked all the way, got ourselves lost wandering round a housing estate. That is, Esther wanted to savour the pleasure of walking along a pavement and admiring the sophistication of other people's television aerials so she got us deliberately lost. When we finally made it through the school doors, I thought we'd stick out like a pair

19

of daft tweedy green thumbs. But no one seemed surprised that we were wearing our uniform from The Dales and not the navy-blue stuff they have here.

Mum made us.

'Better the wrong uniform,' she said with an encouraging smile, 'than no uniform. At least it shows you're trying.'

What kind of logic is that?

The first teacher we found was limp but kind. 'Not to worry,' she said. 'You better pop along to Mrs Craske's office when you've a free moment.'

'Mrs Craske?'

'That's it. Secretary and R. E. Like as not there's a few bits and bobs left over from the lost property sale.'

'We got to wear somebody else's clothes?' said Esther. 'Second-hand? Yeerghk.'

'There's no point in wasting people's money when times are tight, is there?'

I wished she hadn't said that. It's almost as if she knows how hard up we are.

Starting at a new place when you don't know anybody, when your uniform's wrong, when your voice is wrong, and when it's not the beginning of term, is vile and mega-kill horrible. At breaktime, Esther looked out for me and hung around pretending to chat, just so she wouldn't look like a complete no-hope social outcast.

Even when we'd dragged two crumpled navy skirts out of the cupboard in Mrs Craske's office, I didn't feel I blended in any more than I do with my family in the bungalow. I couldn't understand half what the other kids were saying. They couldn't understand me either. They giggled whenever I opened my mouth to ask Mr McCluskie a question in English.

At the Dales, I used to be quite good at English. The Dales is all-girls and so exclusive you had to sit an exam to prove how educated you were before they'd even let you in. This place is mixed in all senses. Still, I'll hand it to Esther. By the end of the second day, she was mixing pretty enthusiastically, though not with the squeaky little lads from her own year.

'Boys of my age,' she said dismissively, 'Are just so immature.'

So she was getting herself noticed by the big dudes from two years ahead. On our third day, she started a fashion fad, rolling over the waistband of the droopy navy-blue skirt to show off more of her long languid legs. She dangled her nasty pass-on cardi over one shoulder, like it was a slinky silk scarf. The dudes gawped. The girls too. Then began to imitate.

A death in the family

But as soon as we've bundled ourselves down the steps of the school coach and into the rural wasteland, glamour antics have to cease. Sugarbeet, potatoes, and crooked oak trees aren't impressed by that kind of thing. And nobody can look alluring when they're striding down a muddy track, then wading through the waist-high nettles.

When we slouched into Belle Vue, Mum had a face as long as an extending ladder.

'Esther,' she said. 'My dear. My darling. I don't know how

21

to say this. I'm terribly sorry. But something really bad has happened.'

How could anything worse happen than already had? I knew at once that someone had died. I thought it must be Dad because he wasn't slumped, staring into space, in his usual place in the broken sun-lounger. Immediately, I wondered how I'd find the appropriate words to write this up in the chronicle of our sad times. Luckily, the words 'grief', 'despair' and 'bereavement' flashed across the VDU screen of my fine literary mind.

But hang on a tick. Why did Mum only say, 'Dear Esther'? Why not, 'Dear Hannah'? Useless though he may be, I think he's supposed to be my Dad too.

'It may well have been a heart-attack,' Mum went on. She was very near tears as she put her arm protectively round Esther's shoulder to hug her. The slinky wrap slipped off and fell to the worn lino where it looked like the horrible blue cardi it was.

'It's Mister Swarzenegger,' Mum said with a choking gulp. 'Actually, it happened early this morning. But I didn't like to tell you before you left in case it upset you so much you couldn't enjoy your day at school.'

Enjoy? Whoever enjoyed a day at that sort of school?

'He's over here.'

Relief flooded through me like warm tea with two sugars. Through Esther too. I could tell from the way her face changed to a lop-sided smirk when she saw it was only Mister Swarzenegger Mum was on about.

'Oh *him*!' she said. 'That's all right.'

Mum said, 'Look dear, I put him in this little box for the time being.'

No shortage of useful cardboard boxes in our household at that time, though the one that Mum had chosen was not exactly 'little', but a socking great grocery carton which had previously contained Esther's entire life collection of footwear. And before that, washing powder, 10 pkts. × 1.2 kg, Euro size 2, biological *and* biodegradable.

A bit like tiny corpses in the hedgerow. They biodegrade.

So, just by the way, how come all *her* shoes and things have turned up, and been put away in the creaky wardrobe and my worldly possessions are still a.w.o.l.?

Poor Mister Swarzenegger's corpse looked insignificantly small, sadly vulnerable, and very dead, as it lay in its outsized make-shift coffin.

Mum said, 'If it was a heart attack, it would have been quite quick and painless.'

So who was she fooling?

'They don't usually live very long, you know. Two years is quite a good innings for a guinea-pig.'

Personally, I suspect that he died of starvation and neglect. Esther's been so busy trying to get a sneak preview of my chronicle that she's been taking almost no notice of Mister Swarzenegger.

However, it was no time to search for the fault-lines in my beloved sister. First, we had to see to the deceased.

Or rather, *I* had to.

Esther didn't want to look at him, let alone pick him up. So she sobbed on Mum's shoulder and managed to produce three tiny tears which were so false they were practically dry, just like artificial snow.

Well done, Ess! This cunning ruse saved her from having to do anything personal about Mister Swarzenegger's little body.

Her grief was short-lived. Once I'd transferred him into a container of a more suitable size (a 200 tea-bag carton) and we were outside looking for somewhere to bury him, Esther's tears completely failed her.

'I never liked him much anyway,' she said as we tramped through the nettles into the woods behind Belle Vue. 'There's so little you can do with a guinea-pig. I always thought they were weird parents to give me Mister Swarzenegger when I'd specially asked for roller-blades.'

We heard a muffled scuffling in the undergrowth. Esther grabbed my arm. But it turned out to be grim-reaper Dad.

The reason he hadn't been in his usual place on the sun-lounger staring out at the nettles as they lapped up against the windows, was that Mum had sent him out to see if he could dig a hole for us. But confronted by the great storm waves of brambles beyond the nettles, he gave up, nodded at us over the prickles, then scurried indoors.

'Gone to resume normal activity of non-speaking look-out man,' said Esther.

I stamped and kicked till I'd made an opening through the brambles and down to the earth. Luckily it was quite soft. I scraped out a guinea-pig size hollow with a kitchen spoon. We laid Mister Swarzenegger to rest.

'Dust to dust, ashes to ashes, into eternity Mister Swarzenegger dashes,' I chanted.

Esther seemed entirely satisfied with my prayer.

The other two sisters

We'd just about finished the burying business when we met two other girls in the wood. Or rather, I did, for once she saw I was getting on with it, Esther rushed on ahead. I was surprised, specially as they too were having a pet funeral. One of them was scraping a shallow hole in the earth under the trees, just as I had done.

'We're burying a kitten,' she said. The fluffy, black and white corpse was not much bigger than the late Mister Swarzenegger. 'She was but three weeks old.'

This grave-digger was fortunate in having a proper spade rather than a wooden mixing spoon. The other girl, who seemed to be older, was sitting like a princess on the dry leaves watching, not lifting a finger to help. Something familiar there.

They both wore coarse brown aprons, down to their knees, droopy black stockings and black ankle boots. They had rather weird hair, long and lank as though it hadn't been shampooed for at least a week.

I wanted to seem matter-of-fact, as though burying pets is as normal as taking a shower.

I asked, casually, 'So what did she die of?'

At first neither of them would answer. They glanced

25

uncertainly at one another. Then the digger said, very sadly, 'She was less than a month old. She'd only just learned to lap milk by herself.' She began to weep into the folds of her apron, more tears and wetter ones, than Esther had managed to squeeze out. 'It was a tragic and unexpected accident. That's how she passed away.'

The sitting-down one said, 'That's all smoke and gammon. You know full well it was Father stood upon her. Trampled her to death in a rage.'

I gasped. Even if bankruptcy had been a contributory factor in Mister Swarzenegger's fatal attack, at least our Dad hadn't done it on purpose, not as far as we knew.

'Yes, it's true, but Father did not do it deliberately,' sniffed the younger girl, as though she knew what I was thinking. 'For no father, however wicked, could do such a thing as that.'

'He could and he did,' snapped the older, sitting-down girl. 'Now Ada, stop that snivelling. It's time we were on our way.' And she held up her arms and waited to be picked up from her tuffet.

The younger one finished patting down the musty earth, then pulled up her sister and heaved her round onto her back.

'Home James, and don't spare the horses!' cried the piggyback rider, tapping her sister with her hand as though she was whipping her pony. They trotted away down a path between the brambles and disappeared round a dark holly bush.

Weird or what?

Just imagine if I had to carry Esther about! Sometimes it

feels as though I do. But the burden is mental rather than physical.

As soon as we got home, Esther went off to rummage through the packing cases to see if she could unearth our portable TV set.

I helped Mum get the tea.

Dad, on the sun-lounger facing out to the gathering dusk, said morosely, 'She'll never get it to work.' It was as though, just because he's failed so badly, the rest of us have to as well. 'Not without an aerial she won't.'

It was odd to hear his voice. He hasn't spoken so much for ages.

Mum said, brightly, 'Oh, but she might. Be worth a try.' She's always trying to jolly everybody along. It might be quite annoying if you were married to her.

I said, 'We met two girls in the wood.'

'Well now, isn't that nice? Are they local?'

Esther stormed back in, irritated. 'Found it. Plugged it in. But it's all blurry like a snowstorm.'

'Top marks for trying, Esther,' said Mum. 'Dunkirk spirit. That's what your granny always said.'

Dad didn't say anything else. But he looked a bit smug, because of being right about the telly not working.

A short while after that, my Mrs Tiggywinkle went missing. I couldn't find her curled up in any of the usual places she liked to be. She didn't meow at the kitchen door. She wasn't there every time you walked into the kitchen, entwining her soft body round your ankles in the hope that you might feed her. And she wasn't sitting on the bathroom window-sill staring intently at you as you cleaned your teeth, willing you to let her in.

She just simply wasn't anywhere. It was much worse than the sudden demise of Mister Swarzenegger. At least with a corpse you know where you are. But when someone in her prime just disappears into thin air, it's eerie.

That night something small and leggy crept out from between the hairy blankets and scuttled across the top from my bed to Esther's. And it wasn't a cat.

Esther gave a little squeal. 'Eek!'

'It's only a friendly spider,' I said.

'But it's in our beds.'

I trapped it in a tooth-mug and put it outside. It's not that I'm really braver than her. It's just that it's best to save your fear in case something worse than a free-range spider comes along.

THREE

Autumn leaves

When the trees start staring

On Saturday, just to annoy me because of the spider business, Esther said, 'D'you suppose Mrs Tiggywinkle might have been savaged by some wild creature?'

There's loads of animals out in the woods. We hear them at night, screeching and howling and wailing and jumping about on the corrugated tin roof. Mum says not to mind, it's only dear little bunny rabbits and friendly barn owls.

Esther said, 'And probably a few bears and black panthers too.'

And Mum quickly said, 'Stop it, Esther. Don't talk like that. You'll only encourage her to have more nightmares.'

The walls are so thin that I only have to have a slightly bad dream and wake with a quiet gasp or a small shout and they know all about it.

Esther narrowed her eyes so they looked foxy and hissed softly so Mum couldn't hear, 'Even a young vixen could probably prey on an inexperienced urban cat. Have you thought of that? And if Mrs Tiggywinkle were to be attacked, d'you suppose she'd have the sense to find her way home?'

I know she wouldn't. She's old (well, nearly as old as me which is very old for a cat), and a bit deaf and not very bright. They got her for me from the Cat Rescue place.

Typical that.

Esther got given Mister Swarzenegger, new from the pet shop. I got a second-hand cat.

Since becoming my cat, she's been used to the soft under-belly of suburban life. Now she's disorientated by the move, and culture-shocked by the wild life, and she wasn't very aggressive to begin with.

So the vision of her lying somewhere in the hostile countryside unable to crawl home to me, was easy to conjure up. It spurred me into action. That's because, unlike Esther, *I am an animal lover*. Yes, Esther, if you're reading this.

I went outside to smash down some nettles in case my beloved Mrs T. W. was lying, injured, in the undergrowth. And I called her name.

Esther decided to come and help. I'd like to think it was because she was beginning to feel sorry for Mrs Tiggywinkle, if not for me. But it was really because she still couldn't get a decent picture on the telly even though she'd balanced it on the draining board with the wire stretching across the sink, and jammed a metal coat hanger into the aerial socket at the back.

We couldn't find the garden shears we used to have. Surely the bailiffs didn't take those too? So Esther fetched the kitchen scissors that Mum used to use to snip the rind off bacon (in the days before we were so hungry that we'd eat anything, including the rinds round the rashers). I found a hefty big stick and we snipped and thrashed and flattened.

'Hey, this'll make a nice space,' said Esther. (Obviously, the exercise had done her good.) 'Next summer we can sunbathe out here and have barbecues for all our friends.'

'*What* friends?'

We changed tools because Esther said the kitchen scissors were hurting her fingers. So she gave them to me and took a turn with the stick. Really it was because she could see that hitting is easier and a lot more fun than snipping.

All the time we were out there, I had a creepy feeling we were being watched. I said, 'Do you get that feeling, Ess, that they're looking at us?'

'Who?'

'The trees. Like they're staring?'

'You're nuts,' she said.

I pointed out to her the sad, saggy, bogeyman eyes on the grey trunks of the oak trees.

'That's not an eye! That's a scar on the bark where a branch has fallen off.'

Perhaps it was the three derelict cottages then, that were spying on us? Those poky peeky little windows were like beady prying eyes.

Esther said, 'You heard what Mum said. You'll give yourself even more nightmares if you go on like that.'

So I tried not to look over at the cottages. Or the eyes on

the trees. But when you've definitely decided not to look at something, it's quite hard not to. And suddenly, I couldn't help noticing a faint shadow rising in a spectral cloud out of the crooked chimney of the nearest cottage.

Somebody had lit a fire. Probably not a spectre. But a tramp, or a homeless crusty. Better still, a sensitive poet seeking tranquillity and solitude. When he realised I too was writing an important chronicle, he'd invite me to participate in interesting chats.

I have decided not to mention this to Esther. She'll either tell me I'm loopy or else take over. If there's an unattached man in the vicinity, she'll claim that this sad chronicle of our sad times was all her idea anyway and she's the creative protagonist.

I snipped away at nettle stalks and then I definitely saw a foggy shape at one of the windows. We were definitely being watched. But no sooner had my eyes noticed it, than it seemed to move away from the window.

On the Feast of Saint Michael and All Angels

'Mum?' I said, when we went in. 'You know you said no one lives down this lane any more?'

'Yes, dear, I know I did, but I was wrong. There's a couple in the cottage. I saw smoke and was worried the old thatch might have caught on fire.'

'All by itself?' I said.

'Haven't you heard of spontaneous combustion?' said Esther scathingly.

'So I popped over to check.'

Esther said, 'Praise be! Mum's Neighbourhood Watch days aren't over after all!'

Mum said, 'You'll never guess! It's two sweet little old ladies!' She seemed pleased, which is odd because I distinctly remember, back in our Buccleigh days, her saying that if she had to go and check up on one more old lady who'd set her burglar alarm off, she'd go crazy.

Yet here she is doing it again.

'They've been there all along. And apparently, the custom round here is never to start lighting your fire until Michaelmas is past.'

'Michaelmas?' Esther said.

'Saint Michael's day. It's their economy, to save fuel. They're as poor as church mice.'

I said, 'Did you ask them about Mrs Tiggywinkle?'

No, of course she hadn't. Mister Swarzenegger may be big-scale tragedy. But my poor Tiggywinkle is hardly worth thinking about. Typical. Esther always get the attention.

Our neighbours, Mum says, are two sisters, Miss Lily Hoggin and Miss Ada Hoggin. 'Poor old dears. I should say they're at least ninety, if they're a day. They're a bit confused. Seemed to think I should know their father. He was quite well known around here. I'm not clear why.'

I said, 'I'm going to ask about Mrs Tiggywinkle.'

'Well please don't upset them, will you, Hannah?'

'Why should I do that?'

'They don't seem particularly pleased we've moved here.

They've got some rather old-fashioned rules about visiting. I think they value their privacy.'

I said, 'But I'm only going to ask if they've seen Mrs T., since you forgot. No harm in that, is there?'

And I thought, How could you have a *rule* about visiting someone?

But Mum was right. They do.

I went over to their cottage. I pushed open the gate. The wood's so rotten it's soft and squishy like a trifle sponge. I thought the whole thing was going to come crumbling off its hinges when I touched it. I went up the path which is green and slippery with moss and tapped on the door, politely, like Mum said I must. I waited. Nothing. Knocked again a little louder.

I knew they must be in. There was still that drift of smoke above the thatch. I saw a shape up at the dormer window in the roof. It looked more like a young boy than an old lady. He moved back when he saw me.

So poor Mrs Tiggywinkle, if she's still alive, out on her lonesome ownsome for another night.

I stepped over a low hedge onto the flowerbed under their window to take a look in. I heard laughing behind me. I jumped away. I was trampling on their flowerbeds just like those horrible journalists did when they were trying to get photos of Dad. I felt guilty. Mum warned me not to cause trouble. I hurried back down the mossy path to the gate. It was all white and freshly painted.

Beware! Children at play

A group of children were in the ladies' garden, playing on the grassy patch behind the cottage which still caught the evening light. Dancing and prancing in the low sunbeams, they seemed distant and golden, yet they were close enough for me to hear them.

And what a racket they made! Enough to waken the dead. Didn't they know this is the countryside where it's meant to be calm and peaceful? Country oicks. Rural yobbos.

Didn't they know about not upsetting the old ladies indoors who had strict rules about visiting?

Apparently not. Two of them were romping about, hiding in the big leaves of the rhubarb plant. The boy with red cheeks was jumping out at the smaller ones in a silly childish way. He looked too old for that sort of thing. One of the girls was sitting beside a bush carefully plucking off rose-pink berries into her apron. They were gooseberries. Every so often, the boy darted back from the game and said something to her. It looked as though he was checking she was all right.

Another girl was unpegging linen off the drying-line. She folded each piece into a wicker basket.

I knew her. I knew them both. Ada, who'd dug the grave and her sister with the stumpy little feet sticking straight out, who she'd carried on her back, who pretended to whip her like a horse.

Ada saw me hanging over the gate. She perched the full washing basket on her hip and came over. The other children went on roaring and yelling and whooping. They had no toys, not even a football, but they seemed to be having fun.

'Good evening!' she waved to me with a friendly smile.

'Gosh. Hi there,' I said. 'Didn't reckon you lived right here. Just close. It's kind of weird.'

'I was born here. We all were, except our Humphrey. Mother and Father were still working up at the Hall then. Did you have an order for her?'

'A what?'

'Some linen to be washed? Mother's very quick. Dropped off Monday, delivered back Wednesday. Sixpence a bag. A penny extra for the blue.'

A woman's voice was calling them in. The boy with the rosy face gathered up the gooseberry-picker in his arms and ran with her indoors. The little ones followed like baby chicks. So did I, but not fast enough.

The cottage door closed in my face as I reached it. I scrambled up onto the milk-churn propped by the front step and pressed my face to the window. I expected to see the children gathered inside. But the glass was cobwebby and clouded with green mildew. It was hard to make out anything except a single figure on an upright chair by the fading fire. Not a child. Just an old woman who wouldn't come to the door when I knocked.

But anyway, it might have been my imagination. Esther says I'm nuts.

Pussy cat, pussy cat, where have you been?
So I had to wait another day before I got a reply and Miss

Hoggin would open the door. I made Esther come over with me just in case.

'Just in case what?' she smirked.

'Just in case nothing.'

'Scared the old biddies might be witches?'

'Course not,' I said. 'That'd be stupid.'

There was some rustling and creaking and the door was opened just a crack and a little face peered round. Of course I recognised her at once, just as she'd recognised me by the gate yesterday. But how could Ada's chubby face, so pink and blooming, have changed into this withered, yellowing old apricot? Mum said they were old. She looked so frail that the breath of a single sneeze could blow her clean away.

Perhaps the weight of clothes she was wearing helped hold her down, a bright knitted pom-pom hat, like a tea-cosy, pulled down over her forehead, a flowery nylon pinafore over layers and layers of wool jumpers.

'Er. Hello. Er Miss er Hoggin,' I began. 'We're from next door.' Was she going to ask us in and offer us fifty pence and a piece of chocolate if we'd sit and talk, like the rich old ladies in Buccleigh Gardens did?

No she was not.

'Yes dear, we know perfectly well who you are. And we enjoy watching you at play. We love the sound of little children.'

'Personally,' Esther muttered under her breath, 'I don't consider cutting down acres of stinging nettles counts as *playing*!'

'Reminds us of when we were young. Well-behaved lassies, are you? Good to your mother?'

'Yes I think so,' I stammered.

'Ada! Ada! What's going on out there?' Another cracked and ancient voice called from inside.

'It's the little folk from over yonder.'

'Mind they don't step indoors. They're bound to carry mud on their boots.'

The door opened a crack wider. I could see into the kitchen. Gloomy and dank. It made Belle Vue seem like the estate agent's dream. The ceiling sagged low in the middle like the underneath of a hammock. The other old lady was sitting stiff as a ramrod on a chair beside the fire. She too wore a woolly rainbow hat, also an overcoat with a bald fur collar and lots of jerseys stuffed under it. Her face was grey with wisps of hair clinging round like ancient cobwebs. Her stumpy feet in hard black boots stuck straight out in front like a wooden Dutch doll's stick legs. There was something very odd about those legs.

Then I realised. It was obvious. They didn't work properly. She was lame as a duck. Always had been. Ever since she was a girl.

'Close the door, Ada! Close that door. You ninny. Why do you let all the heat escape! There's no sense burning good fuel just to warm the clouds. They can do that by themselves.'

It seemed to me that the rush of cold was coming out of the kitchen, rather than into it.

Miss Lily's eyes were sharp as razors. She saw me and there was nothing frail about her voice.

'Well Ada?' she said to her sister. 'What is it they want from us this time? What about our tea? We haven't time for all this idle gossip.' Then she said directly to me, 'It is not our normal custom to receive calls at this time of day. We retire early for the night. However, since you're here, speak your piece.'

I said, too loudly because I thought she might be deaf, 'I'm ever so sorry for interrupting. It's just that I was wondering if you'd seen a stray cat? Well, she's not really a stray. She's mine. She was all right for the first few days after we moved. But now she's gone missing.'

Their electric kettle, balanced on the mantelpiece with its wire straining past Miss Lily's pom-pom hat, began to boil over. Steam billowed out. Miss Ada shuffled over from guarding the door against me, switched off, unplugged, and carried it towards the table. It seemed to be a great effort. She propped herself up at the table with one hand and began filling the enamel teapot so slowly you thought it would take forever. Her hand wasn't steady. Her aim would never score the bull's eye.

'So I was wondering if you'd seen her about? She's a really sweet cat. I had her for my seventh birthday from the cat home. And you know that seven is meant to be a lucky number. Just like cats are supposed to be lucky, aren't they? Black with white front paws.'

Miss Ada shook her head and the bobble on top wobbled. Most of the hot water missed the teapot.

'Now don't go making a mess on that table, Ada. You'll spoil it.'

The table was covered with a plastic lace cloth so stained it looked way beyond being spoiled. Swirls of steam fogged up the windows.

'Well *I* certainly haven't seen any stray cat,' snapped Miss Lily. 'I see all I need to see from my window. And I can tell you I have seen the gamekeeper about. And he is not keen on cats. Shoots them on sight, does he not, Ada?'

Miss Ada began mopping at spilt water with the corner of her overall. Didn't she know, that nylon is not very absorbent material? That's why they use it for waterproof anoraks.

As the steam cleared, I saw a fine black cat curled up on a knitted blanket in a cardboard box right under Miss Lily's chair.

'Oh!' I said, surprised. 'So she *is* here!' I darted in. It was definitely her. Beloved Mrs Tiggywinkle with white front paws. She opened one eye to give me a sullen stare but made no effort to recognise me as her owner.

'No, no, no!' said Miss Lily. 'You are *much* mistaken. That's *our* pussy cat. We've always had a cat, haven't we, Ada?'

Miss Ada was having another bash at filling the teapot.

'Why yes, I believe so, Lily dear. If you say so.'

'We always kept animals. Mother had the geese, d'you remember? First the eggs, then fattened them and sold them at Christmas.'

'And didn't I have a little pussy of my own who died?'

Miss Lily began flapping her hands at me as though shooing away a fly. 'You know you should not have come right in without being invited. Off you go now! We're happy you're around but in future, Miss Ada and I would rather you don't call when it's our tea-time. Nor our dinner-time. And we dine at midday.'

'But this is *my* cat,' I said. I could hear the shrill whine in my voice beginning to take over.

Miss Lily wagged a knobbly yellow finger at me. It looked like a dried banana from the health food shop. 'Now my girl, I hope you're not a trouble-maker. We're not going to regret having you in our neighbourhood, are we?'

Esther waited impatiently on the front step. 'Come *on* Han,' she hissed, and dragged me out by the arm.

'Whew!' she said as soon as she'd got me outside, and the door was closed. 'How could you *bear* to go in there!'

'What d'you mean?'

'Breathe in that terrible pong! You're probably infected with it now.'

'What pong?'

'I dunno. Mouldy bread full of germs? Old flesh on old bodies? Viruses of the past? It just smells disgusting and old.'

'Didn't notice,' I said. 'I was looking at Mrs Tiggywinkle. I'm sure it's her.'

Esther must have heard the whine in my voice changing gear into a choke in my throat.

'Sorry about that, Han,' she said and gave me a hefty, but well-meaning thump on the back. 'Mean old cronies. Still, at least it's better than finding she's been mangled by wild beasts of the woods, isn't it?'

'Suppose so,' I said glumly.

'At least you know she's safe and sound.'

'Yeah, in the *wrong* house, with the wrong people.'

I didn't go straight back to Belle Vue. I went for a stomp on my own through the brambles and the deep litter of dead leaves and I listened out for the voices of children playing. I didn't see any gamekeepers.

I wasn't out long, but when I got in, scratched and somewhat bleeding but only superficially, Mum was in a big stew. She nagged on about where on earth I'd been, and how it was nearly dark and anything could have happened to me.

'If only,' muttered Esther. 'She's off her twig.'

I'm sure Mum wasn't really worried about me. She's more worried about other things. I made a big mistake in telling her so, rather loudly.

'You and Dad have only lost your status, and his business, and some money, and a house. If you'd lost the *only* friend you had in the *whole* world, like I have, you'd *really* know what suffering was. Then you'd have something to worry about!' I said. Well, I more sort of screamed it.

Dad blinked and turned his sun-lounger back towards the dark window. Mum said I was making a lot of unnecessary fuss about nothing.

'But Mum!' I wailed. 'They have no right! Mrs Tiggy's *my* cat!'

'Maybe your cat by name,' muttered Dad from the other side of the sun-lounger. 'But I've noticed that it's mostly your mother who bothers to feed her.'

'What would *you* know about it? I wouldn't have thought *you* ever notice anything, just sitting there all day!'

'Hannah. Please don't be rude to your father,' said Mum. 'Anyway, cats are like that. They make up their own minds, settle where they choose.'

'They *lured* her over there. Thieving cat robbers.'

'Now Hannah, try not to be selfish about it. Even if that is Mrs Tiggywinkle you saw, remember, those poor old dears have probably lead a very hard life.'

'Hard life? You joking? Not Lily, that's for sure. She never lifts a finger. She just sits about waiting to be carried!'

'So if you can't even find the charity in your heart to let them enjoy the company of a cat, I don't know what kind of daughter you are.'

Mum used to take my side in arguments. What's got into her? 'You're *all* against me!' I said. 'You hate me being part of the family.'

'Come on, please let's not go on arguing,' Mum said. 'Now help me lay the table for supper, there's my good girl.' She put out her arms to give me a hug. But I don't want to be her good girl. I pushed past.

'No thank you!' I snarled. 'I'm not hungry. I don't want any supper.'

This is a lie. I am starving. That walk back from Hungry Hill gobbles up calories. I'm always starving. Maybe I've got worms? We learned about them in Biology and Human Science last week.

'It's always the same. Spuds. Spuds. In the rest of Europe, they give boiled potatoes to their pigs. Pig food! I am sick to the back teeth with spuds.'

I storm out of the kitchen, slam the door behind me. In the bedroom I fling myself down in despair. This is a silly thing to do. The mattress is so lumpy that it fights back when you land on it. The springs spike you in the ribs and poke holes in the valuable journals you may have hidden under there.

'I hate it here, I hate it here,' I roar and I beat my fists into the dusty pillow. But even as I say it, I know it isn't quite as straightforward as that.

Later on, Esther brought me a plate of mince and potatoes with a blob of margarine. The potatoes were cold so the margarine didn't melt. But I ate most of it anyway.

Mrs Tiggywinkle, that treacherous feline, came back to her real home in time for a late supper snack, my leftover mince. She left again as soon as she'd wolfed it down.

On Saturday afternoon, Miss Ada Hoggin was seen doddering creakily out of her door, down her path, towards Belle Vue.

Dad caught sight of her first.

'Looks like the natives are growing restless,' he said before he got up and took himself out to the shed, just so he wouldn't have to speak to her.

Now where's the charity in that?

FOUR

Martinmas

When it's time for tea

Mum watched her from the kitchen window. 'Yes,' she said. 'Definitely coming over this way.'

What a local excitement. Better than sitting around wishing we were going out. Esther and I craned our necks over the sink to get a good view.

Mum said, 'I think it's the younger one.'

I said, 'It couldn't be the other one. She can't walk.'

She was making her way down the winding path between the trees, hunched like a gnome, prodding her way purposefully with a stick. She wasn't very steady on her legs.

'What can she want? I do hope she's not in difficulty,' said Mum. She hurried to open the kitchen door so that the old lady needn't be kept waiting outside.

I don't think Miss Ada has very good sight. She certainly didn't see the open door. Or else, she had no intention of coming in that way. She struggled on, right round the bungalow, through the tangle of plant-matter Esther and I had chopped down. She reached the lean-to plastic porch.

We haven't used the front door since we got here. It's blocked up with stuff. Mum frantically began heaving the clothes-airer and the tea-chest out of the way. 'I don't think it's going to open,' she said. The key wouldn't turn. She sent me to find the vegetable oil. I dribbled some into the lock. We wiggled the key about.

We got the front door open. Miss Ada was waiting expectantly the other side, with a smile like a Raggedy-Ann doll.

'Miss Hoggin!' said Mum, greeting the old lady so warmly that she practically crumpled her up into fragments like a crushed crisp. 'Is everything all right?'

'Why, good afternoon to you, Mrs Broddy. And good afternoon to you, Esther. And good afternoon Hannah. Such a pleasant afternoon.' Pleasant? It was mizzling grey drizzle out of a November sky.

Mum said, 'Is there a problem? Can I help you?'

'Why no, I don't believe so.'

'No, of course not. Please, come in.'

Miss Ada already was in, nosing her way down the hall passage. The smell of ancient mould that Esther complained about, hovered round her like a swampy mist.

She was dressed up like someone going to a birthday party. Instead of her tea-cosy hat, she had a velvet Alice bow holding back her wispy hair. She had on white lace mittens, several necklaces of pearls, glass beads, and plastic poppits, and four different china brooches pinned to her cardigan front. She opened the first door she came to. A cupboard. She moved on and found what door she wanted. The sitting-room, or it might have been if we'd got around to clearing it. At the moment it's still the dumping place. Piles of books on the floor, bundles of curtains waiting to be taken up or let down, Mister Swarzenegger's empty cage with a layer of his old bed litter because Esther hasn't cleaned it out.

Mum tried to persuade her out. 'I think you'll find it's really much warmer in the kitchen,' she said loudly and clearly as though talking to someone who was not only ancient but also deaf and daft as two posts.

'Thank you, but no. It is always pleasanter to sit in the front parlour when one is returning a call.'

Mum said, 'I was just worried you might find it rather draughty in here.'

Two of the panes of the window are cracked. One was like that when we rented the place. Dad broke the other. Mum started to fuss around moving things to make it look tidy. I didn't see the point of this.

Miss Ada lowered herself on to a chair heaped with unsorted washing, mostly boxer shorts and socks of Dad's.

'Good ventilation, Mother always said, is one of the prerequisites to good health.'

Mum said, 'The girls are just about to make some tea. Aren't you?' she added forcefully, making tea-making signals at us. 'So I hope you'll stay?'

'Why indeed, that is why I have called. So there is no need to twist my arm.'

You'd have thought that with all those business dinners of Dad's, Mum would be quite good at small talk in sticky social situations. But when we came back in with the tea, she was floundering.

'Seed cake!' Miss Ada said, bright as a chatty bird. 'Now that is a very pleasant and popular comestible. A slice of seed cake at tea-time. Mother used to make it. Though what type of seed, I have no idea.'

'Ah, tea!' said Mum, as though surprised, or perhaps just relieved, we'd come back and not skived off like Dad. But her relief was cut short when she saw we'd made the tea the usual way. In chunky mugs, with messages on them. *Under Gardener* (Mum to Dad when he had the Buccleigh Gardens patio laid for her.). *For the Biggest Mug in all the World* (Esther to me for my last birthday.) *The Greatest Lover in All the World* (Mum to Dad again, don't know when.)

As a distraction, Mum said, 'Oh dear, we seem to have run out of biscuits.'

Who was she fooling? She hasn't bought biscuits for weeks.

'My sister, Miss Lily, asked me to inform you that we have always lived pleasantly,' Miss Ada burbled on. 'Even if circumstances have sometimes compelled us to simplicity. She reminded me to tell you not to let outward appearance deceive you. Her own trials have naturally brought restrictions to both of us. Dear Mother. It's such a pity you never met her. You didn't, did you?'

'No,' said Mum. 'We only moved here in September.'

'Then you couldn't have. She passed on just before the drinking fountain was unveiled.'

'Ah. And when was that?' said Mum as though she really wanted to know.

But Miss Ada moved on. 'Truly as I live, Mother really was the cream. And so very nearly a lady. We always had saucers. Before her marriage, Mother worked up at the Hall.'

'Really?'

'Indoors. Never out. That is where she came by her nice ways. She passed them on to us.'

Esther was using the lid of a crispbread tin as a tray. A tea-bag was swimming like a fat brown lady in each mug.

'Saucers?' Mum mimed at us, urgently rolling her eyes as though we could magic items of crockery out of thin air.

No saucers. No biscuits.

Miss Ada was mystified by the size of the mug and by the tea-bag which kept bumping her nose. I don't think we match up to her level of pleasantness. However, at least she didn't seem to notice the picture or read the message on her mug. (Esther had given her the greatest lover one that Mum gave to Dad.)

Mum said, 'I hope you can manage with that, Miss Hoggin. It's difficult moving house and getting settled properly. Not everything's turned up.'

'Although my sister and I have endured a number of small misfortunes, that of house-removal has never come our way. As Mother said, "Three moves are as bad as a fire."'

'Indeed?' said Mum.

Esther began having hysterics into the sleeve of her sweater. 'Ever been to a mad hatter's tea-party before?' she giggled in a whisper.

I thought it was sad rather than funny.

Miss Ada took three more slurps of tea, and decided it was time to leave. 'Why, I do declare,' she chirruped, 'That it's half past four and not a bone in the truck!'

'Thank you so much for calling, Miss Hoggin. Now, will you be able to see your way? It's practically night.'

'If I can't find my own way home after all these years, then I'm a dead duck,' she said. 'But just to be on the safe side, perhaps your daughter will see me over.' She grabbed hold of my elbow and held it tight so there was no getting away.

Mum put the torch into my hand. The battery's practically flat so it makes a feeble light like a sick glowworm.

'Not to bother with that fiddly-faddle, Mrs Broddy,' said Miss Ada. So we shuffled off, arm in arm, through the wet dusk and her feet did seem to know the way, despite the darkness, and seemed less wobbly than before.

Mrs Tiggywinkle met us half-way and began twisting in and out between Miss Ada's ankles, like she used to twist round mine when she was my cat.

'Dear little puss.' She bent down, quite agile now, to pick her up. I shone the torch so she could see and in its watery light, I saw her face melting like candlewax, and reforming till her grey saggy cheeks became round and full. Then her wispy hair thickened, grew dark, and tumbled to her shoulders in ringlets. The girly velvet bow on top of her head stayed where it was. So did Mrs Tiggywinkle, purring in her arms.

Ada squeezed my hand. 'Oh Hannah, I do hope we can be firm friends. I would so love to have a friend beyond the circle of my family.'

'Me too,' I said.

I went with her as far as the white gate.

'Will you come in and say good day to my sister?' she said. 'I have told her about you. And I would so like you to meet Mother.'

But in the moment that I hesitated, because I wasn't sure then if her mother really existed, Ada changed her mind. 'No. On reflection, best not. Father does not care for the disturbance of visitors.'

Bit like my dad.

I skip home through the dark, excited. I have a special friend. Of my own. That nobody knows about.

Followers

Mum feels sorry for them. She says they're a lot worse off than us. She keeps finding things to give them. Old blankets that turned up when she did some more unpacking. Some of the green tomatoes she got extra cheap in the Friday market because she bought so many. You line them up along the windowsill and they're supposed to ripen in the sun. But it's the wrong time of year for sun. Which is probably why they never ripened in the first place.

But I took them over anyway. And I asked Miss Ada, 'Who's the boy I saw upstairs?'

'Boy? There's no boy. Just we two and our cat.'

Miss Lily, upright in her chair beside the fire said, 'Humphrey, I dare say she means.'

Miss Ada said, 'Aah yes, Humphrey.'

I said, 'Does he live with you?'

'Not any more. He's just a memory. They all are. Only the tough ones survived. But I dare say he must come back from time to time.'

I gave them the green tomatoes, even though they didn't really seem to want them. They mostly eat white sliced bread. They have it delivered. The mobile shop comes down the lane once a week. Everything you buy from it is stale.

Esther said to me, 'Has it ever occurred to you, Han, how peculiar it is that they never married? Neither of them?'

'No,' I said. 'That's because I'm not man-mad like you.'

She's not the only one. There's other people like Esther at school whose only topic of conversation is who fancies who, and who's going out with who.

'Spinsters for a life-time!' said Esther. 'A nightmare. I'd have killed myself before that.'

It isn't as though they were ugly. I know you can't tell now. All old people are ugly on the outside. But when they were young, from what I've seen, they were quite pretty.

Esther said, 'Next time you go over on one of your mercy missions, ask them about it.'

So I did, though not as crudely as Esther would have.

I said, 'Miss Ada, is it true that you've always lived here, your whole life?'

'Why yes, dear.'

Miss Lily by the fire said, 'You know very well we have.'

'Did you never want to live anywhere else? Get away from here and see the world?'

Miss Lily said, 'Why should we? This is our home. We see the world well from here.'

Miss Ada said, 'We were here with Mother, until she passed on. And the good Lord has seen fit to keep us in good health to be with one another.'

I said, 'Didn't either of you ever want to get married?'

It was almost as if I'd said 'bum'.

Miss Lily pursed up her lips and looked into the fireplace. 'We neither of us saw any need for that kind of thing. Not after we saw what Mother went through.'

Miss Ada held the door for me as I pulled on my carboot sale wellies. Mum's getting quite good at sniffing out bargains for us. But it's best not to wonder whose feet used to be down in the dank dark rubbery depths before mine.

'Besides,' said Miss Ada in a low voice. 'My sister has never been very keen on the company of men, she says they do so clutter up the place with their legs and their boots and everything.'

I thought of our Dad on his sun-lounger, right in the middle of the kitchen. And even before his troubles, like last Christmas, trying to get breakfast in bed for Mum, tripping over himself, scattering black crumbs everywhere as he scraped

the toast he'd burned, dropping the teapot lid, then the sugar
bowl.

'Yes, they definitely do.'

After the green tomatoes, it was some blackberry jam she'd
tried to make. But there hasn't been enough sugar so it hadn't
set and needed eating up. I had to take over a jar of it.

'Tell them to keep it in the fridge,' Mum said.

They haven't got a fridge. But I took it anyway.

I asked Miss Ada, 'When you were young, did you ever go
out with young men?'

'Go out with?'

'To have fun.'

'Why yes indeed. At harvest time, we were all out there,
girls and boys, men and women. Mother packed up a picnic
for us. Everybody lent a hand. Everybody that could. We'd
ride up on the haycart coming back in the evening. Not Lily
of course. She stayed home and kept the fire going.'

'I mean,' I said, and searched my spell–check brain for the
word that she would understand, 'I mean, did you ever go out
courting?'

'Mother didn't hold with us having followers. She didn't
care for us to mix. She said it was vulgar, and we were above
that sort of thing.' Miss Ada lowered her voice till I could
hardly hear. 'But really it was because of Father. People in the
village did not approve of his habits. And besides, it wasn't
necessary to mix. We had, right here, all the company we
needed.'

Even though we were whispering on the doorstep, Miss Lily could hear us.

'Ada!' she called and looked at her sister with an eye like a darning needle. 'It was not as you say. One of us had a follower. An uncouth lout who sat right here by the fire with his feet on the fender, whistling indoors as though he owned the place.'

Miss Ada flapped a fly off the table with a dirty tea-cloth.

Outside, I said, 'There must have been other young men, nearly as nice as the one Lily didn't like?'

'Perhaps. If it hadn't been for the war. They all went off, you see. Only a few came back. Never enough to go round. Mrs Pardon, the midwife who lived in the cottage opposite, knew of a charm to make a person fall in love with you. She said it always worked. But by then, I had made my decision.'

'What decision?'

'Concerning my sister.'

'Yes?'

Miss Ada's faded blue eyes began peering into the past.

'It was one harvest time set my mind,' she said. 'Lily wanted to come with us. And two boys jeered and name-called when they saw her riding up on the cart.' Miss Ada clenched her knobbly old fists as though she wanted to hit out. 'And they fell about clutching their sides when she tried to stand upright and was little taller than a circus midget. Humphrey said he would fight them, but we stopped him.'

As she described it, I almost felt I could see it happening, could smell the dusty wheatfield, share Ada's anger and Lily's humiliation.

'So after that,' Miss Ada sighed and dropped her hands, 'I resolved I would not go looking out for marriage till she was wedded first. But there not being enough fellows to go round the healthy girls, no-one was going to look at a cripple. So we stayed together. And very happy we have been.'

FIVE

Advent

Such happy turkeys

At the Low School, excitements are so thin on the ground that they've been preparing feverishly for weeks now. Carol sheets designed. Festive banners painted. Blobs of cotton wool blu-takked to all the windows. How many more pretty decorations can you make out of old foil and painted egg-boxes? It's like being back in Nursery. Mrs Craske asked Esther and me to try to find some nice evergreens to take in to deck the school hall. She means decorate.

She must know that the trees along our lane are simply swathed in ivy, like they're all muffled up for winter.

'Christmas! Bah humbug!' I said. 'She won't catch me dragging bunches of leaves all the way to school just to drape it round the walls. I'm not a Pagan.'

When we sloped home, weary-footed from the walk, sore-voiced from harking through another carol concert rehearsal, the atmosphere inside Belle Vue was definitely different, though it wasn't exactly Christmassy.

Mum was standing in the kitchen spattered with blood and she was smiling, not just one of her tight I'm-being-so-cheerful grimaces but as though she really meant it. It's been ages since she's smiled like that. It lit up the kitchen like twinkling fairy lights. At least, it would've done if there wasn't so much blood about. Very unseasonal.

Mum was wearing white rubber boots. They were splashed with dark red too.

Dad was nowhere, the sun-lounger unusually vacated. A white, red-spotted overall lay over the back of it.

Esther and I both had the same terrible thought at the same terrible moment. Esther said, 'Mum! Where's Dad?'

'Your father?' said Mum. 'How should I know? Round the back maybe?'

Esther ran out to check. Yes, he was intact. Slumped on a stump of wood in the shed holding a piece of rotten wood in his hands like Hamlet with the skull. Or so Esther described it.

'Guess what?' said our malign maternal parent, still grinning. 'Got myself a job!'

'A job?' I said. I thought, undertaker's assistant? Or one of Herod's wicked helpers?

'What sort of job?' said Esther.

I said, 'I thought you told us there *aren't* any jobs round here.'

'There are if you ask and persist. I'm gutting turkeys. Started this morning.' She was terribly pleased with herself. 'Just over Hungry Hill. Towards The Sandpits. There's a poultry farm.

Hundreds of happy little turkeys. Free-range. Well, not very free. But free enough. Kettle's on. Better go and wash.'

So, we're gobbling down a lot of turkey at the moment. Never the soft succulent breast. Always the nasty bits that don't sell. Tough turkey fists, and knuckles and knees. For a family that thinks it's hard-up, we're not doing so badly.

The only problem is: Mum's smell.

Disgusting. Gizzards and turkey poo.

However hard she scrubs her hands, they pong bad.

'Like Lady Macbeth,' said Esther, again showing off her wide literary range.

'What?' I said.

'Shakespeare. You'll know when you're older.'

Turkey-gutters at *Contented Turkeys* wear a uniform like surgeons in an operating theatre, including rubber gloves and plastic bath-caps. Mum used to have lovely hands, manicured once a fortnight when she had her hair done. Not any more.

With her first pay packet she's been to the auction and bid for two bikes. Rusty old bone-shakers. No gears. Spazzy pedals. Rock-hard saddles. But two wheels each. That's what counts.

'So now you've no excuses to keep missing the school coach,' she said.

I've accumulated a lot of late marks, not always accidentally. I thought she wouldn't find out.

She's also bought wine for Dad. None of your cheapo screw-top stuff. This is posh French, with a date on the label and a proper cork made from the bark of a Spanish cork tree.

'Ideal accompaniment for *casserole de dinde*,' Mum says.

She's put candles on the table for tea. Dad doesn't deserve it. He hasn't said thank you. But then, come to think of it, nor have we about the bikes. Mum's the sort of person you just take for granted.

The bankrupt house-father

Coming home from school ought to be good. But it's getting more difficult every week. All day long, I'm thinking about the moment I'll be out of the classroom. It's claustrophobic. I'm straining for the sound of that last buzzer. Checking my time-table to see how much longer to endure. Break-time and four more lessons. Then breaktime and only two more lessons. Then only one more.

In the olden days you weren't forced into education like this. If I'd lived a century ago, I could have been shot of it by now. Once I was twelve and had passed my Standards, I'd have started work. Out on the fields. Picking stones. Bird-scaring. Or maybe I'd have been a milk-maid or a house-maid.

When the last buzzer's gone, there's horrible hassle in the cloakrooms, shoving and bickering and people tossing your kit over the coathooks just to see how you'll react. Then the scramble for the right coach. Then the ride up to the crossroads, with the ones on the back seats smoking and snogging, and the ones on the nearly back seats setting off fire-crackers. Then Esther and me scrabbling in the dark in the empty barn where we leave our bikes. And the long pedal back to Pegg Bottom.

The comforting image of Being Home which keeps me

going all through the day is never the same when it really happens. Dad is not a good houseparent. He doesn't begin to think about it till we're actually falling in through the back door, knackered and starving. That's when he drags himself up and starts to scrape out the cold ashes from the grate, goes out to the shed to fetch in dry wood, begins to clear up the breakfast mess.

No wonder his business went bust.

What does he *do* all day?

Mum says he watches the robins marking their territory.

When she was being our mum, before she turned into a turkey-gutter, it was better. Mum knew about Coming Home Time. She always had tea ready on the table. If you were in a grump and said you didn't want anything, she wouldn't force you. She'd just be there, patiently available, if required.

Sometimes, I like ruminating back over the old life, just simple everyday things, like coming home for tea. One day, I remember, I brought my posh friend Katy home unexpectedly. Even though Katy's got a tennis court and her father is a bank manager, she didn't have a mum like mine. When Katy saw the table all set out with the flowery cloth, and the plate of honey sandwiches, she was just gob-smacked. 'How did your Mum *know* I was coming back with you?'

I said, 'She didn't.'

'But she's put out all this special party food.'

'That's not party stuff. That's just tea. We always have it.'

'Every day? Wow.'

But you never know how lucky you are to have something till you haven't got it any more.

Mostly, thinking about the past just makes me sad. It's so long ago. Four months is in another age.

I empty the sludge of cold tea-leaves into the sink. Esther fills the kettle. She reminds me that tea-leaves block up the U-bend and that makes Dad swear.

I look in the fridge. No milk. Esther looks in the bread-bin. No bread either. But we're not supposed to swear. We make tea and drink it black. We each pour ourselves a bowlful of damp corn flakes. I eat mine with a blob of condensed milk. Esther puts hot water on hers.

Our Dad is useless. He just hasn't a clue about caring. By the time he's coming in with some wood and starting to get the fire going we've lost interest.

'Tea in pot, Dad,' says Esther.

We go to our freezing bedroom to do homework. *And* to get away from him. Gloom is as contagious as the plague.

Mum's been to the auction rooms again. She bid for an old card table. Nobody else bid for it. We have to share it. Esther's drawn a chalk line across the green baize to mark the middle. If any of my books stray over the line, she nudges them onto the floor. They get damp from sucking up the condensation.

I try to dash through my Maths, harum-scarum. I want to get it finished quickly so I can get over to see Miss Lily and Miss Ada. Their past is better than my past or my present.

They never ask me to sit down. But they don't seem to mind if I perch on the side of their kindling box and stroke

Mrs Tiggywinkle and watch Miss Ada getting their tea. There's a scattering of black dots, like grape pips, in the corner of the room. I think they must be animal droppings.

Maths was about Co-sines. I don't understand them. I took the book through to Dad. He was staring out of the window. He can't still be studying robins, not in the dark.

'Co-sines,' I said.

'Better ask your mother,' he mumbled.

'She won't be in for hours.'

'Ask your sister then.'

I wouldn't ask Esther about Co-sines if she was the last mathematician on earth.

When Mum eventually came home she was too tired to think about Co-Sines.

I said, 'Why can't Dad go out to work instead of you?'

'Because he's –, oh Hannah, you know perfectly well why not. Don't go on about it.'

'Does being a bankrupt mean he's not even *allowed* to work?'

'It means there's no point. He's not allowed to keep his earnings. Anything he earned would have to go to the trustees. Towards paying off his debtors.'

'You mean he can't ever work again?' The thought of Dad cluttering up the kitchen for the rest of my life doesn't inspire confidence.

'You get held in bankruptcy for at least two years, probably three.'

Even two more years of having to walk round him seems like infinity.

'He ought to get out. I bet he could gut a turkey just as well as you. Couldn't he go to work and pretend to the judge that he wasn't?'

'That would be dishonest. It's better this way.'

Hm. Doesn't seem it to me.

'And besides, Hannah, he's under a lot of stress at the moment.'

Aren't we all?

Food for the poor

Mum did quite well to talk about bankruptcy. She still gets freaky about certain words. Revenue. Tax Year. Debt recovery. She'd ban them if she could. But fundamentally, she's still the kind-hearted and thoughtful person she always was. How she had a daughter like Esther I don't know.

She's asked me to pop over with another of her offerings for the Misses Hoggin. This time it's a cooked casserole of, guess what?

Wow! Turkey stew! She's told me to say she's cooked too much for the four of us and there's some left over. I know perfectly well that she's specially made enough for them too.

I made Esther come with me. We put on our smelly secondhand wellies.

It was the correct hour for visiting. I tapped. Miss Lily's voice said, 'Come in.'

Their door doesn't fit properly. It's warped. You have to pull on it, and lift at the same time. They draw a heavy curtain against the draughts across the inside. I got all tangled up in it and had to fight my way through. They were in their usual places, Miss Lily upright by the fire waiting for her tea, with her tawny-coloured turkey-skin hands folded on her lap, Mrs Tiggywinkle snugly purring in the cardboard box, and Miss Ada in her nodding pom-pom hat, propping herself up by the draining board in the dark corner with the wet patches all up the crumbly wall, greasing sliced white bread with a skim of margarine, just enough to stain it yellow. Floppy bread and sweet milky tea. They always have the same thing, midday and evening. Probably breakfast too. They obviously don't care for tomatoes. They were still in a line on the windowsill, green as ever, not a hint of red.

'Good afternoon, Miss Lily. Good afternoon Miss Ada,' I said, and nudged Esther for her turn.

'Good afternoon Miss Lily. Good afternoon Miss Ada,' she said.

Miss Lily's name first because she's the elder.

'We just dropped in for a moment,' I began, but stopped short when I noticed the crust of the last slice of bread Miss Ada drew from the plastic wrapper tinged with mould. And there were little black mouse droppings actually on the table today.

'Come on in then, if you're coming in,' said Miss Lily tetchily. 'Wipe your boots properly. We don't want mud all over the place.'

Their kitchen floor is made of mud. It's been flattened and beaten till it's smooth, with some rag-rugs laid on top. You'd hardly think a little more mud off my wellies would make much difference.

I never sit down on the edge of the kindling box until they invite me to. But Esther's more gutsy than me. She just moved straight in, pulled out a chair, flicked the mouse-droppings off it with a tea-towel and sat herself firmly down in front of the fire, picked up the poker and began prodding at the sulky flames while I did the handing-over of Mum's offering. Doesn't Esther know that you should *never* stir up the fire in someone else's home unless you're asked?

As soon as I set Mum's casserole down on their kitchen table I saw Miss Lily's face begin to do the melting thing. Like hot candle-wax going backwards. The wrinkles fade, the pale paper skin begins to glow, the cheeks grow rosy, then the wispy white tufts of hair bounce into corkscrew ringlets. Only her sad little boots stay the same.

Ada is over in her corner scrubbing muddy potatoes in the stone sink. She turns and says, 'How thoughtful of you, Hannah.' Her face is melting back to youth too.

I nudge Esther. 'Look!' I whisper. But she's too busy interfering with their fire to notice. 'Mother will be pleased. Especially with Father presently indisposed.'

'Indisposed?' What did she mean?

'He is unable to seek employment.'

'Ada! You are not to gossip about private matters which do not concern the neighbours,' ordered little Lily from the fireside. 'You know Mother doesn't care for it.'

There was a loud thump from upstairs, like someone falling

66

out of bed, then a subhuman roar like an angry ogre.

It was the indisposed Mr Hoggin. He began to come down the twisty staircase. His feet arrived in the kitchen first, in thick knitted stockings, then his legs in woollen breeches, then the wheezing stinking rest of him.

He stood in his kitchen, red-faced, red-necked. He filled every damp cranny with fury. Even the cat was terrified and dashed past my legs to escape. His eyes were blood-shot. His sandy hair was all messed up and standing on end. 'Food!' he roared. 'Where's my dinner? Does a man have to wait all night to be fed?'

I wished I could hide myself in the folds of the curtain hanging by the door. I didn't dare move. I hardly dared breathe. I glanced at Esther scowling into the fire. She didn't seem at all bothered about Mr Hoggin crashing about. I signalled to her from behind the curtain. She made a Come-On-Let's-Go-Now face at me.

Mr Hoggin sat clumsily down at his table, knocking over a stool so that it fell onto a sack of potatoes. He saw the casserole I'd brought.

'Ada, what is this?'

'It's a gift, Father. One of our kindly neighbours brought it over.'

Mr Hoggin slammed his fist down beside Mum's favourite blue Willow Pattern dish so hard that the lid rattled.

'So it's charity now, is it? They believe we are fit for the poorhouse? Do they think I'll accept patronage?'

'Please eat, Father.'

'We accept nothing from folk who look down on us as though we're paupers when they're little better themselves.'

'But Father, they mean well,' said Ada. 'And it's decent food.'

'Don't you sell me a dog, girl. Get rid of it! Go on with you. Give that rubbish to the pigs. You think I will lower myself by accepting that?'

'Please don't,' Ada, began. 'Let Mother have it. Look, here's something better for you. Gammon and potatoes.'

But he forced her to take our stew outside anyway and throw it in the trough. When Ada came back with the emptied dish, Mr Hoggin hurled it out through the open door. I saw it fly right past me. It landed in the yard and smashed into bits.

Mr Hoggin lurched across the kitchen and reached out to slap Ada across the side of the head. She tried to duck but not in time. Then he went back to the table.

Lily, helpless in her chair, couldn't protect her sister. Mr Hoggin took no notice of her, except to growl, 'And you, useless girl, can't you see the fire wants feeding?'

Ada set in front of him a soupdish piled with vegetables and a slice of gammon. As soon as he was face-down to it, slurping noisily from the spoon, Ada signalled to us to leave.

Outside, I started trembling with the terrible excitement of being so near that angry man.

'Did you see it!' I said to Esther. 'Did you see it? How he slapped her?'

'He?'

'And how they changed?'

'Well, it's good that somebody's pleased with turkey stew.'

'Not the stew. I mean, what happened to them, how they change? Of course, they don't *really* change.' I wanted to reassure her. 'Only the outside of them. They're still the same people inside, young or old.'

Esther said, 'The really old one's definitely not as grumpy as before. It must be very draining to be so disabled. But the Ada one, she's quite loopy isn't she?'

I'm beginning to think she didn't see anything that I saw. Or else she saw it, but differently. Or perhaps it's me that sees things differently.

Broken china

Two days later. I've been over to fetch back Mum's dish. I already knew it was broken. I wasn't surprised when Miss Ada showed me the pieces. She kept on apologising as though she'd broken it herself. 'It just slipped from my hands. That old sink's so hard,' she said. 'I really don't know how it came about.'

Miss Lily croaked with a hint of triumph, 'I warned you to be careful, didn't I now? But she's just a clumsy, stupid old woman. That's her trouble. And half blind with it.'

I said, 'It's all right. I saw how it happened. It was Mr Hoggin.'

'Father? Oh dearie me, it probably was. You see, Father's trouble is drink. But he hasn't always been that way.' She sadly shook her head so the pom-pom nodded. 'What a contented family we might have been if that wretched drink hadn't eaten him up.'

'Sssh, Ada,' said Miss Lily. 'No need to go shouting out our shame for everybody to hear.'

I said, 'I'm not everybody!'

'You know what gossips they are round here!'

'I don't gossip! And anyway, I know everything without you even having to say it.'

Miss Lily looked at me as though I was a sheet of glass. She could see right into me. I knew she believed me.

'I'll get it off my chest and tell you dear,' Miss Ada said. 'It was like this. Father was very often uncooperative. But he couldn't help it. He was a kind man at heart. He turned to drink because he had a big disappointment in his life.'

As she spoke of him, I heard the gate swing open, then the footsteps stumbling up the path, tripping over the chicken-feeder, fingers fumbling at the latch and when it wouldn't lift, the fist hammering to be let in.

He half fell in through the door and would have dropped body-length onto the fire if Ada and the airing-rack hadn't been there to break the fall. They were both so gentle to him, even though he was practically senseless. Lily supported his head in her lap as though he were poorly rather than drunk.

'Sssh now,' she crooned. 'Mother and the little ones are sleeping. Try not to waken her. She's very tired.'

Ada helped him to sit, she put his feet up on a stool and pulled off his boots. She fetched a towel and rubbed his hair dry.

'The waste of it, the waste,' Mr Hoggin moaned.

Ember days of fasting

'Perhaps we shouldn't say it, but it was better after he was gone. We were still hungry but at least we weren't afraid. To be afraid of your own father in your own home, that's no way to grow up.'

'Ada, Father died much later. Don't you remember? Alfred went first. Then Humphrey in France. Father didn't go till a long time later. After the bailiffs had taken everything.'

'Perhaps you're right, dear,' said Miss Ada vaguely. 'It's sometimes hard to remember everything. But I know that so long as we fed him, then he fell asleep.'

She suddenly noticed the broken pieces of china on the table. 'What will he say when he sees?'

'It wasn't you. It was him,' I said. 'And anyway, it doesn't matter. Mum's got another dish. Let me take the bits and I'll stick them together.'

Most of them were there except one little triangle bit. I spotted it behind the cottage on the Hoggin's tip where they'd been chucking out their wood-ash, old bones, broken flowerpots, for decades past. There's some rotting green tomatoes there as well.

The little triangular-shaped china chip had worked its way back up to the surface. I picked it out, rubbed it clean on my sleeve and took it home with the rest. It fitted in with the other bits quite well, even if the pattern wasn't quite the same.

Mum said she couldn't use it for cooking again because the glue wasn't watertight.

'Never mind,' she said. 'It'll look nice with some dried fir-cones and holly in it.'

SIX

Season's cheer with all its trimmings

Hark the owls and foxes sing

With Christmas coming, there's loads more guts to be seen to, so Mum's working overtime up at the Contented Turkey farm. Looks like our celebrations might be a teeny titchy bit better than I was expecting. I already know what our pressies are going to be.

Nothing from Dad of course. But Mum's getting us wellies, new and un-used. They're from the Contented Turkey storeroom.

She finds out all the good wheezes. She'd discovered they're selling off the old-style uniforms. It means we'll have to put up with wearing the *Contented Turkey* logo on our legs. So what? At least we'll go on having dry feet without the risk of someone else's athlete's foot. Esther wasn't exactly thrilled when I told her what I'd seen hidden under Mum and Dad's bed.

'So what were you expecting?' I said.

'A trip to Florida,' she said. It was a sort of joke.

I said, 'And she's got us bike lamps. White and red, front and rear.'

'The glamour of it!' said Esther.

'Better than a kick in the teeth.'

When Mum came in from work, blood-stained and feathery, I heard her say to Dad, 'And what about the old biddies?' There she goes. Always thinking about someone else. Dad should try a bit of that. 'Don't you think we better do something special for them?'

'Like what?' growled Dad.

'Offer them some kind of hospitality?' said Mum. 'Extend our hands towards them.'

'When we're still counting coppers into jam-jars to meet our own the bills?' said Dad. He's such a mean old grumbler. 'You're not lady bountiful of Buccleigh Gardens now, you know.'

But Mum's like a mongrel with a drum-stick once she's got an idea. She doesn't let go easily.

'What better time than now? Invite them over for mince-pies and carol singing.'

'Why?' said Dad sourly. 'What have they done for us?'

'They're our neighbours.'

'That doesn't mean we have to keep busy-bodying round there. And I thought you said your tea-party was a fiasco?'

'I don't busy-body. Hannah pops over from time to time and her sunny nature cheers them up.'

Actually, Mum's got me dead wrong there. I'm not sunny. Deep inside, if only she'd look, she'd see I'm dark and muddled.

And the reason I go over is because it gets me away from Dad's sour mood and the smell of turkey guts. And even when the drunken ogre is there, at least he never threatens *me*.

Dad began to raise his voice. 'Now you listen, Sonia. I don't know if you're still living in cloud cuckoo land or what. But the facts are, you're working your backside off for a below-minimum-wage. We've two school children we can barely afford to clothe. We're both of us practically on the edge of nervous collapse. And now you want to start handing out aid to the poor and needy who've apparently been managing perfectly without you for years.'

Eavesdropping is a bad thing to do. You hear things it's better not to hear. Like parents quarrelling. It brings back that sick feeling. Makes me frightened Dad'll scarper like my friend Natasha's did.

Mum ignored Dad's advice. She asked me to go over to extend her hand of seasonal friendship.

Miss Lily and Mrs T. were cosy by the fire while Miss Ada skivvied away in the corner at the sink. Sometimes, it's almost as if she's a servant working in a separate room. I suppose if you've existed with the same sister in the same kitchen for so long, you have tricks for making yourself feel you're on your own. I ought to try it with Esther. The white chalk line definitely isn't working even though we've extended it across the floor.

'You can't stop long,' said Miss Lily frostily. 'It's nearly our bed-time.' Not even seven o'clock! But if you haven't got the telly, and you can't read, and you're trying to save money on electricity, there's nothing for it but bed. Also, it must take her about an hour to crawl up the fifteen stairs, even with Miss Ada heaving from behind.

'Well, don't just stand there and gawp, girl! Letting all the warm air out. Since you're here, step right in and close the door. I've told you before, there's no sense in burning fuel just to heat up the squire's woodlands.'

There isn't a squire any more. The man who owns *Contented Turkeys* is buying it all up. And the big house has been turned into some kind of residential home. Esther says it's for drunks and druggies. I think she's wrong. If it was, we'd see them trying to escape. We never see anyone.

Miss Ada went on sploshing at the sink, holding one cup at a time under the cold tap and rubbing with a slimy cloth that looks as though it's seething with germs. It makes Dad's style of washing up seem mega-hygienic.

'So. State your business,' said Miss Lily.

'Well you see Miss Lily, I, er, that is my mother, er, our family, wondered if you and Miss Ada would like to be invited for Christmas dinner.'

'I beg your pardon?'

I do wish Mum hadn't made me do this. It would've come better from her. What if they're so confused about dates that they don't bother to celebrate any more?

'You know, the twenty-fifth of December. Because my mum thought that if you hadn't any other plans, you might like to pop over to us. For the turkey and pudding and stuff. Or for mince-pies and singing. And by the way, Dad said he'd think of a way of getting you there,' I quickly added even though he hadn't said any such thing.

'I see,' said Miss Lily, with a dry clicking of her fingers. 'But no thank you. Miss Ada and I have all our usual arrangements in hand.'

Usual arrangements? There wasn't so much as a single card or a sprig of holly in sight. The only slightly seasonal thing is a wall-calendar covered in brown fly-spots. It says *Season's Greetings, Chadwick & Sons. Livestock, Poulterer. Noted for Quality.* It's for the year 1961. There's a picture of a cow standing by a tree.

Miss Ada turned from the sink, her pale blue eyes as bright as when she was young, and said slowly, 'We had some lovely Christmasses when we were girls. You'd have envied us.'

'That's right,' said Miss Lily. 'Indeed she would.'

'Father wasn't *always* the worse for drink, was he, Lily?'

'No. It was only as the disappointments in his life began to mount up.'

Miss Ada said, 'Everybody has their cross to bear in life.'

So what was Mr Hoggin's big disappointment that turned him to drink?

Miss Lily said, '*I* was his cross. He wanted another son, after Humphrey. He got another girl and crippled at that.'

Miss Ada tottered across the kitchen to her sister to put her arms round her neck. 'Oh my poor Lily. Don't say it.'

Miss Lily said, 'It's all right now. You know it is. And he'd go weeks without touching a drop, then do wonderful things to surprise us.'

Miss Ada clapped her hands together. 'Why yes, you're right Lily! Remember the good times. Do you remember when he brought us back the pig's head on the twenty first of December? Shall we tell her?'

'Yes Ada.'

'No, you Lily. You do it so much better.'

They told together.

On the feast day of Saint Thomas

The old faces dissolved. The kitchen was lively with children dancing round the table. The chestnut logs on the fire crackled merrily and Mr Hoggin strode in through the door with a hessian sack slung over his shoulder. He lowered it onto the table and untied the top. The family gathered round and peered in. Coarse pink hairy skin. Two pointy ears. A long snout. A whole pig's head in a sack. It was enormous.

'Fourpence, that was,' he said.

Mother Hoggin was so pleased she gave him a peck on the cheek. She and Ada set about preparing it straightaway.

First, Mother Hoggin took out the eyes. They wouldn't be eating those, though it was the only part they didn't. Then Mother Hoggin sent Ada upstairs for a clean muslin square.

'One of Baby's napkins will do,' Mother Hoggin called up through the floorboards.

The brains came out and were tied in the cloth and boiled. Ada watched and helped with every stage so she'd always know what to do if she ever came by a pig's head again and Mother Hoggin wasn't there.

When the brains were done, Mother Hoggin and Ada spread them out on a bed of mashed potatoes. Meanwhile, they removed the tongue, and boiled it whole. It lay in a dark red curl as though licking the inside of the pan.

The cold cooked tongue was eaten sliced, with raw onion and bread for tea.

Finally, the whole head went into the big preserving pan, filled with cold water to the top so it looked like the poor pig was drowning. Mother Hoggin and Ada carried the pan over to the fire, trying not to slop the water. When the water first started bubbling, the pig's head began to bob up and down like he was learning to swim to save himself from drowning. The head had to boil all night long. Mr Hoggin crept down and made up the fire several times over. And it simmered all morning too. The smell of pork filled the air. Lily, sitting so near, breathed in the best of it. The others, at their jobs outside with the geese and the hens and chopping wood, kept coming back to hang round the kitchen door sniffing. They grew hungrier and hungrier with the smell.

Humphrey went in and asked, 'Is it ready yet, Mother?'

When finally it had finished boiling, Mother Hoggin lifted it out of the pan, drained it and put it on a tin plate. The skull bones fell out quite easily, and those that didn't, Mother Hoggin picked out carefully with a fork.

'It must be ready soon, Mother.'

It still wasn't. Mother Hoggin put another tin plate on top.

'Fetch me a stone Humphrey,' she said. 'Or a tile. Something heavy, there's a good lad.'

He brought in a brick from the yard and an old horse-shoe from the lane. He put them on top of the plate. Then the flat-iron went on top of the brick and the horse-shoe, and then the weights from the weighing scales went round the flat-iron. It had to be left for another three hours to cool down as it was pressed.

Twenty-four hours later, at long last, on Christmas Eve, Mother Hoggin was able to cut it up into succulent glistening slices of pink brawn which they ate with roast potatoes and roast parsnips. The water that the head had boiled in went to make soup.

What a feast for fourpence.

They lived off the pig's head for the whole of Christmas week. And even when the meat was done, it had one further use. One of the tiny bones was washed and stitched into the pocket of Lily's calico apron on the instructions of Mrs Pardon.

'For that's the surest cure as ever there was, a piece of pig's bone, for alleviating any affliction of the lower leg.'

Festivities with Katy

In the end we did exactly what Miss Lily and Miss Ada and Dad wanted us to do. That is: Mum left the Misses Hoggins alone and stopped busy-bodying round them. It was all because my friend Katy's rich parents, all of a sudden and out of the blue, invited us to spend Christmas with them.

Katy's mum scribbled on her Christmas card, '*Do do come! It would be such fun!! Like the good old days!!!!! We've been thinking about you all so much! To have you here with us would be the icing on the cake!'*

'She can't have been thinking that much,' said Esther, inspecting the postmark on the envelope which showed it had only been posted the day before. 'I expect someone else has dropped out.' Esther never much liked my friends.

Katy's parents must know about Mum and Dad's budgeting with the jam-jars, because they've included some rail vouchers for the tickets with their card. They must know how Dad's not allowed to open a bank account until he's been discharged. Mum's earnings and the Benefit go into the different jars. Each one's marked. SCHOOL BUS, SCHOOL DINNERS, RENT, COMMUNITY CHARGE, FOOD, EXTRAS (which is always empty).

Dad said it was extremely embarrassing to be patronised in this way. He said Mum must send the tickets straight back.

I felt my heart freeze. I waited for her to decide what to do. I thought I wanted to go back to Buccleigh Gardens. I thought I was relieved when Mum said,

'Not at all, Graham. Don't be such an old misery. You were saying yourself how we could all do with a change of air. I think it's very thoughtful of them to want to include us in their happy times.'

So I was moderately excited. To go travelling on Christmas Eve. To see Katy again. To have a good moan with her about my new school.

We couldn't set out till after Mum's last shift finished at midday. Esther and Dad and I walked up to the *Contented*

Turkey farm and waited, with the rucksack and the turkey sandwiches for the journey, on the track that leads up to the processing sheds. All the time we were standing there, cars kept zooming up with people in who'd come to collect their orders at the last minute.

The trains (two changes) were crammed with other families. Dad fought his way along to the refreshment carriage and came back with four teas and a crispy chocolate bar to go with the turkey sandwiches. He and Mum both perked up. Dad even smiled when he saw Mum still had some feathers caught in her hair which looked like snow flakes.

There was an announcement to say that the buffet had run out of beer and sandwiches. This got a cheer from some of the people in our compartment. Then they began singing *While Shepherds watched their flocks by night.* It felt quite partyish.

The railway track ran alongside the motorway for a short way. It was jam-packed with slow-moving cars. I waved. I don't suppose anybody saw me. Doesn't matter. It made me feel good. Mum put her head on Dad's shoulder and went to sleep.

Being on that train, we were a safe compact foursome. It was the best part of the whole Christmas trip. The only good part in fact. Once we arrived, we had a really grossly, mega-death stay.

Rich pickings

Mum took them, as a present, a really contented turkey. It wasn't a freebie. She had to buy it. The special thing about it was that she'd plucked and gutted and trussed and stuffed it with herbs and chestnuts herself. It didn't actually have her signature on it, but it had her code-number.

'Oh no!' cried Katy's mother. 'But darling!'

No? What an ungrateful thing to say when you've just been given something. I wasn't going to be saying, No darling, when I unwrapped my pair of white turkey farm wellies. I was going to say, Oh yes. White wellies with a smiling turkey on the side. Just what I've always wanted. And Esther was going to say just the same thing because we'd agreed it on the train.

Katy's mum said, 'Sonia, my dear. What a *shame* when you've gone to so much trouble. But you see, we're having *goose*! And I don't think goose and turkey meld, do they? The trimmings are different. Never mind, I'll pop it into my freezer so you can take it back with you. I'm sure you don't want to see it go to waste. And I'm sure you can use it.'

Mum smiled and smiled so you'd think her face would break. And I saw how her hands were so red and raw like they'd been dunked in blackberry juice and her hair looking like a rook's nest and I wished so much that I could pick her up and take her away from Katy's parents' all-white drawing-room.

Why couldn't Katy's mum have just pretended to be pleased with a stuffed turkey, and then thrown it away when we weren't looking?

We'd brought some school fir-cone decorations too.

'Oh how sweetly quaint!' said Katy's mum. 'But it's a tartan theme for this year.'

On Christmas Day morning, they had a big party. They said

it was for us, with crowds of their neighbours swarming in. They wanted as many people as possible to see them being generous to us. Some of them used to be *our* neighbours. It was strange to be with people you once knew but don't know any more. I kept thinking of tree trunks wrapped up in green ivy mufflers and how I'd rather have them for company.

Esther found their viewing lounge. She sat and channel-zapped through the party.

Katy told me, 'Mummy and Daddy were going to send a donation to Oxfam, but they decided to have you to stay instead. It's a really nice idea, isn't it?'

It's awful to know you're not a real person, just the icing on someone's cake.

Dad's like Esther. Or is Esther like Dad? He didn't turn up for the Christmas morning party either. As the first guests rang the chimes at the front door, he walked out through the conservatory doors. I don't know where he went. For a long shamble round the streets, I guess, to re-live his guilty past. Odd, that. He never goes for long walks down Pegg Bottom lane. He didn't come back in time for Katy's mother's goose dinner with all its special trimmings (blackcurrant sorbet, prune compôte, gooseberry sauce, water cress).

I had a mattress on the floor of Katy's room. She stayed in her own bed, towering above me. But she didn't sleep much. She kept dropping things onto me, books and socks, and presents out of her Christmas stocking that she didn't like. It was meant to be a joke. I tried to laugh.

She couldn't give up her bed to me, her mother told me,

(not that I wanted it) because she needed to be extra well rested before her big trip. Well, that's what her mum said.

'This ski holiday is so important to her, Hannah,' said her mother. 'I'm sure you understand. To help her through her exams.'

All Katy could talk about, when she wasn't throwing things at me, was skiing and the European weather reports. Before, I'd been looking forward to telling her about Miss Lily and Miss Ada. But I decided not to. She wouldn't have understand any of it. I can't think why I was ever friends with her. We have nothing in common. Instead of talking about them, I thought about them. Because of Christmas being about birth, I thought a lot about Lily being the way she was.

Little clicky hip

When Lily was born, she had two dislocated hips. Mrs Pardon, from the cottage opposite, thought there was something up the moment she saw her. She wasn't a trained midwife, or even a nurse, just someone who helped out if called upon. She'd seen lots of babies being born. And Lily didn't seem to her to be the right shape. But since Lily was so small, Mrs Pardon couldn't be quite sure.

'It's been a long hard night for all of us, dearie,' she told Mother Hoggin with a shrug. 'So I may be seeing things crooked when they're straight. Let's have another look when we've all slept on it.'

Besides, there was nothing she could do about it even if the baby did have a problem.

'And like as not, there isn't anything anyone else can do about it either, dear. That's just fate, that is. I dare say she'll even grow out of it.'

Downstairs, young Mr Hoggin had been obliged to mind his son Humphrey for over an hour and prevent him falling into the fire.

Mrs Pardon came down and told Mr Hoggin he had a lovely girl. Instead of being pleased, Mr Hoggin was angry.

Mrs Pardon said, 'But you already have a son.'

'And two sons would have been better. What can you do with girls? They don't have muscles on them. You can't work them so hard like you can a boy.'

'Well, I'm right sure she's going to be ever such a lovely little miss,' said Mrs Pardon and decided there and then not to mention the unfortunate congenital deformity. Instead she made some tea, because Mr Hoggin clearly wasn't going to, and took it up to the young mother in a dainty china cup on a china saucer because she knew how young Mrs Hoggin liked things nice and fancied herself as a bit of a cut above being married to a labourer. When she came down from settling the new baby, she gave some tea to Mr Hoggin too. But as soon as Mrs Pardon had left, he tied Humphrey by the leg to the kitchen table with a strip of rag so he wouldn't toddle towards the fire, and he took some money from the tea caddy and he set out for *The Three Magpies* on Hungry Hill.

To begin with, Lily's legs were fine. Only if you looked under the four flannel petticoats she wore to keep out the cold could you see anything. Even before Ada was born, she was pulling herself up and beginning to walk. The more she toddled about, the more often her soft bones slipped out of place. The more she put weight on her crooked limbs, the more they fixed themselves in the wrong place and grew that way so by the time she was five she could scarcely walk at all.

The feast of Saint Stephen

I've only once seen Miss Lily's feet, naked, out of their boots. I knocked and walked straight in without waiting for one of them to say, come in.

Miss Ada was kneeling on the floor with a tin basin and a piece of flannel and she was washing her sister's feet.

They were short and twisty, with cross-over toes. They looked more like pig's trotters than human feet. They were chafed and sore with the ulcers on them. Perhaps the boots didn't fit properly.

I caught only a glimpse before Miss Ada quickly wrapped them in a towel to hide them.

'Not now, Hannah,' she said. 'It's not the right time for visiting.'

So I went straight out again and we never mentioned it.

Such sad feet. I wish I hadn't seen them.

That wasn't the kind of thing I could possibly have told Katy about.

If we could have, me, Esther and Mum (Dad, too, when he got back from his Christmas day walkabout) would have left straight after the roast goose. But there weren't any trains running. So we had to wait till Boxing Day.

On the journey home, I asked Mum, 'Have you ever heard of dislocated hips?'

'Of course. That's what Esther was born with.'

'Esther?' How could she. Esther was straight and tall, not splayed and twisted.

'No, it must be something different. I think I got the words wrong.'

Mum said, ' "Clicky hip", that's what the nurses in the maternity hospital called it. But they didn't seem too bothered. Oh look, they said, We've got a little clicky hip here. It's when the ball of bone at the top of the thigh doesn't fit properly into its socket. It clicks out.'

I didn't ask any more questions about it but Mum told me anyway. She likes reminiscing about when we were small. It brings back her youth. All the details, over and over. I don't listen when it's the story of birth. It gets too gory and painful.

'So then they called the orthopaedist in. It seemed strange to have a big specialist for such a wee baby. He agreed with the nurses. Congenital dislocation, not hereditary, not very common, and luckily not serious if treated straightaway. She was set in plaster for a month. A nuisance with the nappies. But it gave the bones time to stay where they should. And that was it.'

That night as she climbed into bed without any help from me, I said to her, 'Good night, Esther. I'm really glad you're not deformed.'

'What *are* you on about now?'

SEVEN

Into New Year

Raining and pouring, old ladies jawing

Wet. Grey. Overcast.

There's been a lot more weather about. Rain every day for five days. Thin, cold, seepy drizzle. It's indoors as well as out. It trickles down the chimney into our bedroom in black greasy lines. It by-passes the soot and the three bits of scrumpled-up paper from my homework that I chucked into the grate. It runs out of the grate, silently and sneakily gathers its forces to make its way with new vigour across the lino floor which is on a downhill slope, then collects in a puddle at the exact spot beside the bed where I dropped my tights and school skirt last night.

'It's raining,' I say, picking up my wet clothes and shaking them.

'Great Scott, Hannah,' says Esther. 'You're a genius. I was wondering what the wet was.'

I peer out at the murky morning. 'But it may clear up later.'

'You turning into our own BBC weather forecaster?' Esther

grumbles. She doesn't like conversation first thing.

'Weather's very interesting. In fact, I made a new year's resolution. From now on, I'm including each day's weather in the family chronicle of our times.'

'Hm. Much good may it do you.' She seems to have forgotten how interested she was in my chronicle before.

There's no point in trying to dry out the skirt. It'll only get soaked riding to the crossroads. So I'm putting it on clammy. With any luck, I'll catch pneumonia and won't have to go to school for a few years.

On the way home, we both had to pause for breath at the top of the last hill. The air's so cold it paralyses your lungs right the way down every time you breathe in.

Esther stamped her feet to try to warm them. I gazed out over the sodden expanse of barren fields. It seemed as though we were the only two living creatures left out here. Everything else had died of the cold, or burrowed deep into the earth, or was shivering in hibernation in some cranny in a tree. Or if they were half human, had crawled into their dwelling, pulled tight the curtains against the winter, and were dreaming of hot sun and waving palm trees.

There was no sound except the swishing of the wind through the bent thorn bushes. Then, there was something else out there.

Esther stamped her feet more noisily.

'Ssh!' I said. 'Listen!'

'What?'

'Curlews!' I could hear them from a long way off, their frail high peeping.

'What curlews?'

'Birds. They're coming now. Look!'

Four of them were flying towards us, very low to the muddy field, their long curved beaks as slim as black wires, all of them peeping continuously like a nestful of kittens.

'You can tell the weather by them. If they come this far inland it means we're set for a week of frost and then some easterly winds.'

'What makes you think they're curlews?'

'I don't know. I just know. Lily must have told me.'

'But she never goes out.'

'Yes she does. They carry her out to sit in the meadow when the kitchen floor's being scrubbed.'

Labours of love

I know they're pleased to see me back. Miss Lily actually invited me to draw up the stool and sit beside her.

'Come, warm yourself at my fire, my dear,' she said and patted me on the head as though I was a lost lambkin.

Mrs Tiggywinkle merely glanced up in her usual rude way, blinked her yellow eyes and completely disowned me. Perhaps she and Esther are related?

They never ask where I've been or what I do. They're so incurious about any life beyond their own damp walls. As though nothing anywhere else even exists. What's happening today in Sydney? Or Bombay? Or Washington?

90

Too far away for them even to think about.

There's more reality in their memories. Though I sometimes wonder if they're true. They argue such a lot over the details.

'No no no, Ada, you silly goose!' Miss Lily says. 'You know it wasn't like that. You'll confuse the girl if you tell it her wrong. That winter, we all took with the measles first, then the whooping cough came on after. If you're going to tell it, you might at least tell it right.'

It doesn't matter to me who's doing the telling. No sooner has one of them started to remember, or misremember, than the light grows golden and misty and their faces melt and brighten into the freshness of their youth.

And here we all are in the kitchen with something unexpected happening. There's a kerfuffle upstairs. It's making Ada anxious. Poor little Ada who has to do so much for so many people. And feed the hens. She's more flustered than usual.

'Lily, Lily!' She comes hurtling down the stairs. 'It's Mother. She thinks her time has come!'

I'm so daft I think she means their mother's life is at its' end.

'But that's terrible!' I say. If she's so ill, why don't they send their brother to fetch a doctor? Specially given what happened to Lily.

'Why no, Hannah! Mother would never want to call the doctor in. And waste two guineas she hasn't even got.'

And Lily adds, 'That's if he doesn't have to do anything. Three guineas if he does.'

'But if she's dying?'

Lily is shocked. 'Who said anything about that? What Mother's about to do, she's done five times before. She'll manage again. Mother's due. Even if it's sooner than she expected.'

Ada says, 'Mother thought she wasn't due for at least another three weeks.'

Ada knew how to get everything ready and she's only my age. She's made up her parents' bed with clean sheets, top and bottom. She's folded a third sheet into a small square to lay in the middle. She's placed a sheet of brown wrapping paper under it.

'That's where Mother must lie to be confined,' Ada explains. 'And afterwards, so there'll be nothing unpleasant for Father to find, Mrs Pardon will wrap everything up in the paper and burn it on the fire. Except the afterbirth which she says must be saved and hung on a thorn bush to protect Mother against malignant fever and milk-drought.'

Ada has also got ready clothing for the baby.

'Because it'll get cold. They can catch their death if you don't dress them quick as a flash. And there's the basin and jug all ready to wash Mother afterwards.'

There's another call for Ada from upstairs. I ask, 'What about Mr Hoggin? Hadn't someone better fetch him?'

'Fetch Father home? Gracious no,' says Lily. 'She wouldn't want *him* around. This is women's business.'

The two little ones are out in the yard chasing the hens. I keep them out of the way. Keep myself out of the way too. If Mother Hoggin doesn't want her husband in the house, she wouldn't want a stranger. But then Ada calls me in.

'Mother says to go up and say good day.'

Mrs Hoggin greets me warmly. I'm surprised. I didn't know that someone having a baby could look so ordinary. She's sitting in a wicker chair by the window, the black cat on her lap. That video they showed us at school in Health and Community, with the woman sweating and swearing and grunting must have been exaggerated.

'Oh I am glad to see you here,' she says. 'You help to keep the peace between those two. They're like mud and honey. And another pair of hands to help Ada with the little ones. She's such a good girl. Will you tell her not to send for Mrs Pardon till I say so?'

She clenches her fists tight for a moment and looks as though she has indigestion. It passes and she says, 'Don't look so worried, duckie. It's not half as bad as you think, really it isn't. Believe me, it's worth it every time. You know, I used to think we'd just have the two of them, a boy and a girl, and that would be my limit. But when Lily turned out the way she is, it didn't seem fair to saddle our son with such a burden. Then our Ada comes along and she's such a treasure.'

She clenches her fists again. 'Well, here we go. I better be getting on with it. Busy day ahead. But do you know, I wouldn't give a single one of them back.'

Downstairs, I'm thinking about that educational film with the mother doing all the gasping and yelling.

I say to Ada, 'She's ever so peaceful up there. Is that really how a baby's born?'

Ada looks shy. 'Not for me to say.'

Lily says, 'Our Mother never likes to make a fuss. It's not ladylike. And not with the little ones about. She wouldn't want to frighten them to death. She just holds on to herself and does it quietly.'

Quiet it may be but it goes on a long time. I help Ada get the little ones off to bed, all tucked in together in the big bed all four girls have to share. Humphrey's truckle bed stands on the little bit of space at the top of the stairs under the sloping roof. You can hear the scrabbling of birds in the thatch overhead.

It grows dark. 'And still no little stranger here,' says Lily. I sit with Ada and Lily by the glowing embers till I hear Esther calling me from a long way off.

'Hannah! Hannah! Hannah!' like an owl crying through the trees.

'I'd better go.'

So I went home and it was time for tea. Esther scowled at me across the table which she'd had to lay all by herself.

'Wherever have you been? I was looking for you for ages.'

'None of your business. To get a bit of privacy if you must know.'

'Well you can jolly well wash up.'

I asked Mum, 'When you have a baby, how long does it take?'

'Now there's a funny question, Hannah, in the middle of eating spaghetti' (Spaghetti Bolognaise, turkey-style. Mum's discovered pasta is nearly as cheap as potatoes.)

'Homework is it?'

'No. Just wondered, that's all.'

So after tea, she told me all the same old stuff that she's told us before, the power of love, and eggs and sperm. She always keeps it general and doesn't like answering direct questions about her and Dad.

This time, it isn't procreation I'm interested in. It's giving birth.

'So how long does it really take?'

'Oh, I don't know. Time doesn't always mean much. It depends.'

How could she be so vague about something so important? 'What on?'

'All sorts of things. Like how big the baby is. The mother's state of health. It can take only an hour. But in the past, I believe women used sometimes to be in labour for days on end. Nowaways, I expect they'd do something to speed things up well before then.'

'How long did it take you? Having me?'

'You were easy. No trouble at all. Esther was a lot more difficult. I don't know if it was to do with her clicky hip.'

Mum looked at me very intensely. 'Hannah, why all these questions all of a sudden. You're not, well not – ?'

I felt myself go hot all over. I couldn't look at her. How could she think such a thing? I'm far too young. I haven't even been kissed by a boy. And as for the other things you'd have to do, it makes me feel quite sick.

'Mum!' I said. 'You *know* I don't ever ever want children.

Not even if I adopted them. I've told you that millions of times.' I'm going to do something useful with my life. Having six babies, one after the other, like Mother Hoggin, didn't seem a very useful thing.

'Hannah dearest.' Mum's concerned maternal expression. 'You know you can always ask me *anything* you want?'

'Of course.'

'And you'd tell me if there's anything worrying you, wouldn't you?'

'Yes,' I said. 'Of course.' But I'm not sure I would.

The baby arrived next afternoon. It was a boy. Mother Hoggin was in labour for twenty-five hours. Mr Hoggin stayed away all that time. Humphrey came home from potato-picking on the field, took one look around the kitchen door and decided that this was a women's place and he'd do better to stay outside and sleep in the shed.

'One night in the cold won't do me no harm,' he said gruffly when I took him out his dish of potatoes. Not exactly a grumble. More an acceptance of what a boy had to put up with if he was to behave like a man. Later on that night, he went rabbiting.

I got my first glimpse of the baby when it was less than fifteen minutes old. It was scraggy, like one of Humphrey's skinned rabbits hanging from a nail out in the shed. It had dark eyes like Mr Hoggin, and a pointed foxy face with foxy-coloured hair like Humphrey. It wasn't beautiful but there was something about it that I'd never expected. When you've not seen a newborn baby before, you don't know about the newness of it. Nobody had ever set eyes on this tiny human before last week, before yesterday, even before a quarter of an hour ago.

It wasn't messy and horrible and purple and screaming like on the health video. It was just so perfect, its pale white skin radiating light like a candle. Its dark eyes gazing out like shiny black marbles. It seemed to understand everything about us. The little ones were as awed as I was as we watched Ada bathing him in the sink.

As she patted him dry, she took care round the stump of cord at his belly. Then she pulled on a yellow woolly vest which tied at the neck with dainty satin ribbons. She let me fasten the bows. Even such a tiny vest swamped the baby. Then she wrapped him carefully in a big clean cloth so he was like a boiled suet pudding. And on top of that came a blanket of bright knitted squares.

Ada did the work. Lily, who did nothing, kept telling her more things that must be done.

'And make Mother her tea, Ada. Don't forget. Mrs Pardon says she'll be needing it rightaway. In a best cup, don't forget, with a best saucer to match. Then take the baby back up to her.'

Ada carried the bundle of pudding baby. I carried the bone china teacup. Mrs Pardon was just finishing upstairs. She had a dirty face and a gap in her teeth like a rat but she had cleaned up Mrs Hoggin beautifully.

She was lying back on the pillows in a clean gown with a

neat ruffled collar. She looked so clean she was shiny. In the flickering light from the bedroom grate, even the white china chamber pot under the bed sparkled.

'I'll be off now,' Mrs Pardon said to Mother Hoggin. 'Well done pet.'

Mr Hoggin's return

There's the grating sound of the white gate swinging open. It bangs against the post as it shuts. He's going to ruin everything. He's going to smash up the quiet household.

I hear him pause in the kitchen, speak to his children, then come clomping up the stairs. I know I can't get out of the room in time.

I press myself into the shadows in the corner where the ceiling slopes down to the floor. There's a soft tap on the bedroom door. That's him out there at the top of the stairs. He's knocking to come into his own room. I've never heard my Dad knock like that. He and Mum are like equals. Sometimes they even have a bath together, like kids.

These two are formal.

'Come in Mr Hoggin,' she says. She's going to be upset with him, for going off, leaving her to it on her own.

He comes in, all coy, peering round the door. She smiles back. Then he's cradling the baby wrapped in its multi-coloured blanket in his great rough arms.

'So it's a boy then?'

She nodded.

'Oh, Lordy Lordy, I do love you,' he says. He looks down

into the little pointy face. And I can tell from the way they both look at the baby, then to each other, how much they're going to love him. I wish I'm not here. It isn't my business. It's something very private between them.

He kisses the top of the baby's head before he lies it back in the crib. It isn't really a crib, just a potato basket, lined with felt. He kneels down by the bed as though he's going to say his prayers. He takes her hand and kisses it. There's tears in his eyes.

'Thanks, thanks, lovey,' he says.

I shouldn't be here. But I'm glad I am. It's so beautiful, it's holy. If ever I have a baby, I want it to be like this. It isn't like Mum's description of having me. She never mentioned anything about Dad crying tears when I was born.

Dad said to Mum, 'I was talking to one of the old men down in the village this afternoon.'

'Oh yes?' said Mum, bright and interested.

'That's a change,' I muttered. 'I thought you'd lost the power of speech permanently.'

He ignored me. He's always ignoring me. Perhaps I'm turning invisible.

'This fellow in the pub was talking to me.'

I said. 'You went to the *pub*? Mum, you mustn't let him go there.'

'Hannah dear,' said Mum, laughing. 'What's got into you? A couple of hours in *The Harrow*. It's hardly a den of iniquity.'

Dad went on. 'They were telling me about the old dames

from next door. How they were actually born right there. There was six of them altogether.'

'Yes, incredible, isn't it?' Mum agreed. 'To think of a family of eight, all squeezed into that tiny hovel.'

'It isn't a hovel!' I said angrily. 'It's their home and it's beautiful.'

'Yes dear, of course it is,' said Mum, patronising.

Dad said, 'Apparently, none of the others survived long. All buried before their time.'

I said, 'Not even the new baby?' He mustn't die before he was named. Ada said you couldn't go to heaven if you weren't baptised.

Esther said, 'What are you on about? What new baby?'

Dad said, 'One son killed in the fourteen-eighteen war. The rest died of measles. Or did he say whooping cough? All except for those two. They must be tough as old boots.'

I burst into tears. I didn't really know why. I ran off to bed.

Esther shouted after me, 'Well, that's a canny new way of getting out of washing-up!'

I heard Mum say, 'Don't wind her up. You know she's going through a moody patch.'

EIGHT

Lent

Gone fishing

Weather report: More of the same. Rain. Overcast. (It *must* be fine in the morning.)

I set the alarm to go off at six on the dot. It frightened the life out of me. Deepitty deep. Deepitty deep. Deepitty deep. On and on, right through my skull. I put it under my pillow last night.

I grappled with the pillow trying to find it. Have to stop the deepitty-deeps. Don't want Esther waking. She'll be angry to be woken on the first Saturday of half-term, just when she wants her beauty sleep.

Seven deepitty deeps and she didn't so much as twitch under the blanket. No movement. Not even a change in her breathing. Sleeping sound as a slug. Brain dead.

I slid to the side of the bed, as silent as a cold draught. The bed springs pinged. I lay still till they'd stopped jangling. If I woke her, she'd want to know what I was up to. I don't want to tell her. It'd spoil it. If I told her it was about a boy, she'd want to come too. If she came too, she'd find out which boy. And she'd tell Mum.

I lowered my feet to the clammy floor. Lino seems to draw in the cold. It's daft wanting to get up so early. Slide back under my blankets? No. I made up my mind yesterday.

Peek through the curtains.

Weather report: rain stopped.

I crept round the bed in slow motion. Not bump into anything and make a noise. I bent down and picked up my clothes in one swift movement. Better get dressed in the kitchen. Just as cold in there but at least she won't hear me.

Tip-toe towards the bedroom door. Last night, I left it a tiny weeny bit open so there'd be no need to turn the knob and push. Far-sighted, heh?

As I slid like a shadow through the doorway, the sleeve of my sweater brushed against the doorframe with a woolly swish. Esther heard it. She started up, nearly awake.

'Hannah?'

I froze. Guilty. Why? For getting up early? Or for trying to do what I'm going to do?

'Hannah? What on earth are you crashing about for? You mad or something?'

'I'm not crashing.'

'You must be. You woke me up.'

'Just going to the lavvy.'

She opened her eyes and peered. 'No you're not. You've got your clothes in your hand. What're you *up* to? Why can't you relax? There's no school.'

'I decided to get up.'

'I can see that. But what *for*?'

I'd have to tell her. 'I'm going fishing.'

She blinked. 'Fishing?'

I nodded.

'You don't know how to fish. You haven't even got a fishing rod.'

'Somebody's taking me. Going to show me.'

' "Somebody"?' She sat up. 'Wow. Who?'

Of course I wasn't going to tell her.

'It's private. And you don't know him.'

'So how come you do?'

'He lives round here.'

'Nobody lives round here.'

'Well he does. I see him in the morning, when he's on the way to work.'

'Well, take care.' Suddenly, big sister was solicitous. 'Will you be all right?'

'Course. He's only young. He's got a crippled sister.'

'Crippled? You're not meant to call people cripps.'

I see him on his own in their garden when he's chopping the wood. I spy on him through the hedge. He said I can go fishing with him. Maybe it won't work and I won't be able to see him. But I won't know if I don't try.

Esther said, 'Where are you going? You should always tell someone where you're going on a date in case it goes wrong and you need rescuing.'

Ho ho. Some likelihood of *her* ever coming to my rescue.

I said, 'It's not a date. He says he's got permission to fish at the lake beyond the big house.'

'The old people's retirement home? Down the long drive?'

'His mother used to work there. So he's allowed to fish.'

'Well, don't do anything I wouldn't do.' What kind of advice is that?

'I'd never want to do the kind of things you do,' I said. 'And *you'll* never understand the kinds of things I do. That's because we've about as much in common as honey and compost, that's what Mother Hoggin says.'

'Who on earth is Mother Hoggin?'

'Nobody you know.'

I creep out through the early morning drizzle. Although we have scarcely exchanged two words with one another, I know he knows that I am waiting for him in the shadow of the holly bush. He comes out of the shed with the garden fork and I watch as he digs through the compost heap beside the rhubarb patch.

I know he is looking for worms. To use as bait. Worms like the drizzle. I'm sure he tells me that. Or perhaps I knew it anyway. He finds plenty.

It's still practically dark. His sandy hair and pale skin seem almost to glow in the half-light. The backs of his hands are covered with freckles.

Esther says she can't stand red-heads. She doesn't know what she's talking about. Mum used to fancy some German tennis player who was so fair he had no visible eye-lashes at all.

Anyway, I don't fancy Humphrey. I like him. I like the way he's so gentle and matter-of-fact with Lily.

There's a yellow brass tobacco tin with our sovereign's head embossed on the lid. He gives it to me to hold as he fills it with the bait. They are wriggling, succulent and the dark colour of ripe redcurrants.

He's very shy. So when we reach the lake, we prefer to sit in silence. Some people don't like being talked to all the time. Besides, when you're fishing you're meant to keep quiet or you frighten the fish. He puts his jacket down for me on the bank. The light slowly grows from the east. It's very mysterious, just sitting there watching while he tries to land the biggest pike in the whole lake.

There's a splash. He points out the ripple of a moorhen coming towards us through the reeds. We're so still it doesn't even know we're there.

And then the mist clears and there's a red sun-rise through the trees, and reflecting on the water. I am so happy I don't want anything to change.

History lesson

Weather: Frost. Ground solid. Pipes frozen. Can't flush the loo. Mum's put a bucket of water beside the loo. We have to chuck it down after we've been.

As soon as we were back after half-term, Mrs Gribbon announced her latest project. They like setting projects. It means they can sit back and rest while the rest of us slog away like child labourers in the Industrial Revolution.

'We're going to cover this part of our course-work using living source material as much as we can.'

Note the 'we'. What she means is 'you'.

'We are going to be asking the older folk, people who actually lived through the period we are studying, about changes they'll have witnessed in their time. In education, transport, leisure-time activities. "Oral history" this type of study can be called.'

Three yobs at the back sniggered. Some boys are gross. No wonder Esther hangs out with mature people.

'As you know, if you've been paying attention, history is concerned not only with the great newsworthy events like armed conflicts and governmental policy-making. It is also the day-to-day minutiae of life. And it is surprising how much we can learn by listening intelligently to what ordinary people have to say.'

One of the sniggerers at the back put up his hand. 'This going out and talking, Miss, is it homework, or voluntary?'

'It is an important part of your coursework. So, once we have planned our questions correctly, as I am about to show you, we will be able to set forth into the locality and put our investigative powers to good use. I think we're going to find it really rewarding.'

They say that when they know we're going to find something dull and unrewarding, like Co-sines. You could hear groans of anticipated boredom from the back row. When history doesn't include bombs and tanks and armed conflict with a high body count, they don't think it counts.

But as for me, I'm really excited. At last, here's something I can do well. Long before Mrs Gribbon finished rabbiting on, I knew who my chosen subjects are. It's obvious, isn't it?

'And don't forget, if you are going out after dark, if you are interviewing someone you don't know well, always go in pairs.'

Ha ha. As though Esther would bother to come with me to visit 'The odorous hamsters', as she's taken to calling them (even though Mum's told her not to).

Now she's discovered the Young Farmers' Friday Evening Karaoke up at the *The Harrow*, she has no free time for anything else.

I had a little sleep through most of the lesson, and tuned my ears in again when Mrs Gribbon put on her summing-up voice which means she wants everything sorted before the buzzer goes because she's gasping for a wee and a coffee.

'Now, is there anything any of you need to ask, or want to have clarified?'

Mandy, who sits at the edge of the class with her back to the wall for security, began whining.

'But Miss, I don't *know* any old people. It's all young marrieds and little kiddies up where I live on the new Briar Estate.'

'What about grandparents?'

'Haven't got any,' said moaning Mandy.

Nor had I. Dad's mother died when I was six. We never knew Mum's mum. But it wasn't going to stop me.

'Well, your parents then?'

'They're not *old*! Mum'd kill me if she thought I was asking her about being old.'

'Nobody's suggesting that, Mandy,' Mrs Gribbon said patiently. 'But she's older than you, isn't she? So her experiences, for example of childhood leisure, will differ from your own.'

'No,' said Mandy firmly. 'Mum's bringing me up just the same as she was. Out of respect for my Nan who died.'

'I'm sure if you put your mind to it, Amanda, you can work out some kind of questions with a modicum of interest?'

Homework

As soon as I started doing it the way Mrs Gribbon said she wanted it, I knew it was coming out wrong. Boring and negative. It made Miss Ada and Miss Lily seem unreal, as though nothing had ever happened to them. They've lived in the same place for the whole of their lives. Never married, never done anything, never been anywhere.

Mrs Gribbon had this check-list we had to work through with our interviewees. It was just crosses all the way through. I bet if I put this in as course-work Mrs Gribbon will say I haven't even tried and give me no marks at all.

Education: Miss Lily: none. Miss Ada: not a lot.

Extended family still remaining in the same vicinity: None.

Holidays: None

Leisure-time activities (e.g. local clubs, visits out): None.

Favourite telly or radio programmes: None.

Experiences of employment or unemployment: None (unless you count looking after your sister for a hundred years

108

as a job, and selling vegetables and goose eggs to passers-by at the gate).

The interview

'Miss Lily, can you tell me if you have seen many changes in your time as a resident of Pegg Bottom?'

'Dear me, Hannah. You'll be the death of me with all your fancy questions.'

'Just try,' I urged.

'Well, they do tell us we're better off with being on The Welfare, don't they?'

Miss Ada said, 'But I don't know what Mother will say when she finds out. "You'll never catch *us* living off the parish". That's what she used to say. "Over my dead body" she said.'

And even when something did happen to them, they argue about how it happened.

'What is the most significant thing that has happened to you?'

Miss Lily says it was having the cold water tap indoors in 1953. Miss Lily disagrees. 'And what use is it? Look at it now, frozen solid.'

Miss Ada says that perhaps it was getting in the electrics.

But that started them bickering about the date. Was it 1969 or 1971? Miss Lily said, 'And besides, I don't care for Ada using that electricity. I'm not sure it's always safe. We're a lot better off with the lamp and the old kettle on the fire.'

It wasn't her that had to trim the lamps and fetch in the wood, was it?

NINE

When the cake was really thin

So many of the things that happened are shameful for them to remember. No wonder they don't like me putting my nose in.

Baby Alfred

When Mr Hoggin's off lubricating his throat instead of working, they often don't get enough to eat. When he comes in, he has to be fed first. That's the only way Ada knows to calm him. Then he falls asleep, just like a baby.

Except that the new baby doesn't sleep. He just cries and cries.

'Because Mother's milk's going,' says Ada. 'She's next to nothing left. Alfred's that hungry. When he cries, it makes Father angry and I'm afraid he'll beat Lily.'

Ada does her best, feeding her brother a little cup of sop off a spoon. It's bread, soaked in hot water with a sprinkle of sugar.

'It only keeps him quiet for ever such a short while,' Ada

says so she gives him a clove ball to suck to try to make him sleep.

Alfred's her favourite but she can see how he's beginning to fade with not getting enough. For once, Mother Hoggin wants to call in the doctor. But they haven't the money. She calls in Mrs Pardon instead.

'If you ain't feeding him right,' says Mrs Pardon, 'His bones won't set and he'll be feeble all his life, just like your Lily. And you don't want that, do you now? So why don't you try giving him a lick of Virol every day?'

'So how are we to find the money for Virol?' says Mother Hoggin.

Miss Lily said, 'But of course she did find a way. You better tell her, Ada, about the time Mother became a washer woman.' Miss Ada said. 'Very well. If I must.'

When Mother Hoggin became a washer woman

When Humphrey got in, he'd always ask, so polite, for he was a lovely boy, 'Mother, will there be anything to eat? And you'd know he was so hungry he could eat the back legs off a donkey.'

Miss Lily said, 'Of course he was hungry! Out doing fieldwork in the wind and rain. Twelve hours picking stones. Paid by the day. Could be laid off at any moment.'

'Course there'll be tea,' Mother Hoggin used to say. She didn't want anyone to think she couldn't provide. 'A knob of a chair and a pump handle.' It was a joke. She meant, 'It'll be the same as usual, boiled potatoes with cabbage.' There was sometimes a little bit of pork but that had to be saved for Father. He had to have the meat.'

Miss Lily said, 'He taught Humphrey how to poach a rabbit. But he couldn't do it himself. Many a night, it was all he could do to grope his way home. And when he didn't find his way back by midnight. Mother would wake Humphrey and send him out to search in case Father had tumbled into a ditch and was drowning.'

Miss Ada said, 'Or freezing to death.'

Miss Lily said, 'That's right. There were sharper winters when we were young. There was a farmer nearby, had a lot of hay-stacks standing, and the crows were pulling the stacks to pieces. So a boy from the village, no older than our Humphrey, was put by the Steward to keep them off. He stood there all day yelling at the crows till he got struck by the frost. Mother found him stiff, near dead, brought him in, saw to him with blankets and hot sand and all she could do and brought him round.'

Miss Lily said, 'That boy, doomed from the start.'

'Harry,' said Miss Ada.

'He died.'

'Just after our brother.'

'Abbeville.'

I wondered where Abbeville was.

At the rear of the cottage there's a separate room, part of the building, but not quite a shed because it has its own front door and its own chimney. It has two windows and dis-tempered walls.

I thought it was their lavatory, that it had the chimney to keep you warm, just like there were radiators in the bathrooms in Buccleigh Gardens.

'Why no Hannah!' says Ada, often surprised by my ignorance. 'Never the privvy right beside the house. That would be injurious to health.'

The privvy is right down the end of the garden path, way past the rhubarb. Scary in the night, not that they've ever said so.

So Mother Hoggin begins to take in other people's dirty washing and the wash-house becomes their life-support system. There's the brick stove on one side, holding a copper wash-tub with a round wooden lid. You light the wood in the fire-box at the bottom, fill the copper with water fetched from the pump, put in the soft soap, with a handful of wood-ash to soften the water, stir in the linen with a pair of wooden wash-tongs, then bring it to the boil.

A copperful of boiling water can't swish the clothes about, or rinse them or spin them at four hundred revolutions a minute. All of that has to be done by hand. There's a zinc bath for the rinsing. It's heavy wringing out big linen sheets or damask table-clothes. You have to take care not to let the ends of the washing trail on the ground.

The children help. The washhouse gets snug and steamy. When the two smallest children have the whooping cough, Mother Hoggin sits them in there with her all day long, so they breathe in the soapy vapours.

'If that doesn't clear their lungs, then nothing will.'

Mr Hoggin pays a pal to catch him a fresh mole. Mother Hoggin is to roast it, the poorly children to eat it to cure them of the cough. But Mother Hoggin tosses it away on the tip.

'We'll have none of that witchery nonsense round here,' she says. 'It's a sensible remedy or nothing.'

Being a washerwoman is hard labour and nearly as low as you can sink. Only cleaning turnips in the field is lower, for then your skirts are sodden right up to the knee from standing in the mud all way.

If anybody calls, Mother Hoggin sends one of the little ones out to the gate to say that Mother is out. She doesn't want anyone to see her flushed face and raw hands. She makes the children do the errand of returning the clean linen, each parcel carefully wrapped in brown paper.

Ada's big brother

I'm over there just as Ada and Humphrey are setting off with all the brown paper parcels piled up on the hand-cart. I'm going to trot along the lane with them and help pull the cart. I hope Ada doesn't guess I'm growing sweet on her brother.

Down in the village, we find a great commotion. A crowd gathering on the green. We elbow to the front to see what's going on. There's a lorry with its tail-gate down. An army officer is standing up with a loud-hailer addressing everybody in so stern a voice that even when you can't understand the words, you feel compelled to listen and agree. Other fine, strong, young soldiers with shiny boots and Blanco-white belts, are standing around as part of the recruitment effort.

Almost before we know it, Humphrey's volunteered. He's joining up to go and fight the Hun.

'But Humph!' Ada cries. 'You're too young. Whatever will Mother say?'

'You'll find out when you tell her,' he says with a grin.

Then Ada's so proud to be his sister when people start shouting, 'Three cheers for the red, white and blue!' and throw their caps in the air. They pat Humphrey on the back and tell him, 'Well done!'

Every member of the family sees Humphrey off to war. Even Mr Hoggin stays sober long enough to wave goodbye from the gate, with Lily perched up on his shoulder so she can get a last glimpse of the splendid khaki figure before he rounds the bend in the lane.

Mother Hoggin's smiling and crying at the same time. 'Come back, come back soon,' she calls.

'Bring us back a parrot!' Lily shouts.

'Bring me back a parlez-vous!' Ada calls.

'What's a parlez-vous?'

Ada shrugs. She doesn't really know. 'But I'm sure it's something they have in France.'

Living history project

'Goodness,' said Mum. 'Whatever's got into Hannah these days? So much studying every night.'

'Rehearsing to become her teacher's pet,' said Esther.

I don't care what she says. Doing Mrs Gribbon's project is turning out to be mega-brill. I'm really enjoying it now. Using all the stuff in my journals. It doesn't feel like work at all. It feels like I'm flying. There's so much material to choose from. I've been so busy. No time to quarrel. So it's good news all round.

I'm keeping in anything that's actually about Miss Lily and Miss Ada, even the stuff about their father going off to see about a dog all the time, because although they don't want the world to know, there's no way they'll ever get to read what I've written.

Miss Ada's practically blind now with her cataracts. And Miss Lily never learned to read properly because of not being allowed to go to school. But to be on the safe side, I'm disguising them, changing their names to 'Violet' and 'Rose'.

Obviously, I'm leaving out all the personal stuff about me and Esther, except when she's really been slagging me off. Also observations about weather. I don't think weather counts as History, except for the winter weather in France in 1917. Humphrey wrote home how it rained and froze and rained some more, and how the birds died of cold and dropped like bullets into the frozen mud, and the soldiers who didn't get blown to bits, had their feet rotting away inside their sodden boots. It was called Trenchfoot. He said, Not to worry. He hadn't got it because he was used to the cold.

I've been up till quite late copying out the sections from the chronicles. I've nearly got to the end. My hand-writing's getting quite wobbly. But at least I know I'll get it done in time.

'Mum,' I said. 'What's Virol?'

She didn't know.

I said, 'I thought you knew everything.'

She laughed. 'Is this really homework?'

'Sort of.'

'Try Dad.'

'Dad doesn't like talking to me.'

'Don't be silly Hannah. Of course he does. It's just he's been a bit under the weather. So would any of us if we'd taken the knocks he's taken. But he's coming out of it. He's a real rock, your father. And don't forget it.'

Dad was in our shed fiddling about with some bits of wood. He's unpacked some of the tools from a cardboard box. Saws and things.

'Mum wants a shelf in the kitchen. I thought there might be a length of wood in here I would use.'

I said, 'I didn't know you could do carpentry.'

'Used to do quite a bit. When I was younger and had the time. Last thing I made was a high-chair for you.'

That was centuries ago.

'Thought I might try and make your mother a dresser, you know, for the kitchen, to put her bits of china on. Don't say anything though. In case it doesn't work out.'

I said, 'What's Virol?'

He said, 'Disgusting, though my aunts used to like it. Thick, brown sticky stuff, in a glass jar.'

'Like Marmite?'

'No. More of a burned taste. Made out of malt. My aunts said they gave it to them in the war, to build them up when they were on rations.'

'Which war?'

'Which war d'you think, silly? World War Two.'

In some ways, my dad is so young. I let him get on with his woodwork. I just hope it doesn't turn out to be another of the knocks in his life. It's the first I've ever heard about him making a high chair for me.

Alfred

The baby died anyway, even though Mother Hoggin bought him his Virol. Mrs Pardon said he hadn't the strength in him to fight a fly.

Ada always used to put him into his crib and kiss him goodnight. Mother Hoggin told her she must go up and kiss him for the last time. His face was quite cold.

When she saw how sweet he looked in his little white lace bonnet, she said, 'Couldn't we warm him up before he goes?'

Mother Hoggin said, 'We mustn't disturb him any more.'

Even when your baby brother has died, the potatoes still have to be peeled, and your sister Lily seen to. When Ada was working down in the kitchen, she felt sorry for Alfred up there on his own, waiting to be fetched away.

She whispered to Lily, 'Perhaps he's not really dead? Perhaps he's just pretending.'

Lily, who hadn't seen him upstairs, said, 'Stop your nonsense

Ada. He's too young for pretending.'

Mr Hoggin came to the door with the hand–cart. Mother Hoggin carried down their baby and they both went off with him for the burial.

Ada thought she missed him more than the others did.

'But then I realised that missing isn't something that shows on the outside. The others might've been missing him more than I did. Funny thing was, I specially missed that terrible gurgling sound of his coughing.'

Mrs Gribbon warned us we'll lose five per cent of our final mark for any work handed in late. I was still writing it this morning when it was due in. I missed the school coach. Had to thumb a lift with a sugar beet truck even though Mum's told us we've never ever on pain of death to hitch-hike. The driver only went as far as the sugar beet clamp on the Yew Tree Road farm. So had to run the rest of the way. Got sweaty. Missed Assembly. Got another late mark.

But, got to History in time, thank goodness. It's second period. Losing five per cent wouldn't be *that* bad since I know I'm going to get quite a good total mark.

We handed in our work. Most people produced half a dozen pages, at most ten. The real swots had printed out on PC's at home so it was neat and professional-looking. Mrs Gribbon likes things neat. Mine looked a bit messy, I'll grant her that. I've been using so many different sized bits of paper. I tried neatening it up by tying them together with some string, and then cutting down the edges to make them all the same size.

It didn't help, not when you're using blunt kitchen scissors. Some bits of my notebooks I've handed in just as they are, with only a few alterations or crossings-out and bits of white paper glued over the bits she mustn't read.

Mrs Gribbon looked astonished when I went up and placed my work on her desk with the rest.

'*The Complete History of the Hoggins*,' I said. I was proud. Like Dad with his woodwork tools out again. I should have remembered what comes after pride.

'Goodness Hannah!' She obviously wasn't expecting quite so much. 'Is this all your own work?'

Well really! I'd hardly hand in someone else's, would I? unless I was a cheat. So I smiled and nodded. More fool me.

She flicked through the top pages. 'Aha, yes, I recognise your somewhat individual and idiosyncratic style of handwriting. Well, let's hope there's quality as well as quantity.'

Drippy Mandy has just about managed one and a half sides, with extra big writing and making all the dots on her i's into round O's. She filled up the remaining half-a-side with soppy drawings of pink flowers and rabbits in sunhats.

'I couldn't think of any more questions to ask my mum,' she whined. 'And anyway, my mum says she's never gone in for havering or gossip.'

TEN

When my world starts tilting

The calm before the storm

Weather forecast:

Something strange and wonderful is happening. A new type of weather. At last. A softness in the air we breathe.

The fields remain dirty beige-coloured. But I can sense the change even if I can't see it. I'm sure I felt the jolt underfoot as the earth tipped on its axis. It's something to do with the spring Equinox. It has to do that so we'll be nearer the sun for summer.

When I asked Esther if she'd felt the judder too, she said I was talking hippy poppycock and had I joined the Druids.

She and I have been trying not to bike home together. We both scramble off the coach at the same time, but I make sure I pedal slowly. Then we don't have to talk and get up each other's noses. But sometimes you can't help it. When she gets off to walk up the last bit of hill, I find I've caught up and we're both plodding along side by side.

I concentrate on thinking about what's going on with

nature. (Esther thinks about the agricultural student she fancies.) There's a strong new smell wafting out of the bank. For months, the only smells have been muck-spreading, silage, rotting straw or the sour smell that foxes give off.

This new smell is sweet like honey, or French nougat.

When I had to get off my bike for the last hill, I saw what it was. Some squat grey flowers pushing up through the mud under the hedge. Mr McCluskie, who teaches English even though he's a Scot, told us that daffodils are the first heralds of spring. He calls them harbingers. Actually he's wrong. It's these drab things. But they're so ugly I guess the poets couldn't be bothered to write about them.

I picked one and ran after Esther with it. She wasn't pleased. She doesn't respond to the miracles of nature like I do.

'Don't *do* that!' she said, pushing me away.

'But *smell* it, Ess!' I urged her and held it under her nose so she could take a sniff.

'Urrgh,' she said. 'It's sickly. Disgusting. Like rotting human flesh.'

I said, 'How would you know what rotting flesh smells like?'

'I can guess.'

'I bet you've never even *seen* a dead person.'

'And you have, I presume?' she said with heavy sarcasm.

I said, 'As a matter of fact, yes.'

'Anyway,' she said, 'You're supposed to leave wild flowers where they are. They're protected. You could be prosecuted for vandalism.' She got back on her bike even though we were only half way up the hill and pedalled hard to the top. I picked a small bunch of the grey flowers, added a stem of dried red sorrel and one crazy white daisy that had come out too soon. I tied them with a piece of dry grass to take to Miss Ada and Miss Lily.

Miss Ada had to put her face practically into them to see what it was I was showing her.

'I picked them specially for you,' I said.

She was much nicer about them than Esther. She accepted them as though they were treasure, then handed them to Miss Lily.

'Aah, yes. Do you remember how much Mother loved the winter heliotrope?' Miss Lily said with a smile.

They began to talk about butterbur and vetch, figworts and spearworts. They remembered to each other how they used to sip nectar from primroses, to clean their boots with the furry paws of pussy willow.

Indoors, the scent of the winter heliotrope becomes stronger. It's like those cheap incense sticks that Esther used to buy. Almost overpowering so that I felt sick. As I watched the pair of pom-pom hats nodding over my grey posy, I was sure they were going to melt. I really wanted them to so I could go back with them. But they didn't do it that day.

There's a new flower. Fluffy white clouds, high up in the hedges, like snow. I leaned my bike against the trunk of an oak, climbed up onto the saddle so I could reach to break off a branch. Close to you can see each starry blossom clinging to the dark spiky twigs. No bad bark eyes staring. It's funny to think how I used to be frightened by the trees.

Back at Pegg Bottom I ran with the spray directly over to the cottage.

When we'd done the 'Good afternoons', Miss Ada peered to see what it was I'd brought her this time.

'Aren't they lovely?' I said because I thought they were. Like a Japanese brush-painting we'd had to study in Art. The flowers dainty against the rough stem.

But as soon as Miss Ada made out what it was, she jumped away as though she'd been bitten by an adder.

'Oh no! Oh Lily, look what she's brought in!' Her voice was all quavery.

Then Miss Lily began flapping her hands like she does when the chimney has a sudden down-draught and smoke puffs out. 'What is the foolish girl thinking of? She ought to know better than that. Make her get rid of it Ada, quick, before it's too late.'

Miss Ada shoved me towards the door. 'Out, out!' she quacked.

I said, 'What's wrong? Where's the fire? All right, calm down. I'm taking it out.' I chucked it onto their tip.

'Those thorn flowers,' Miss Lily said sharply. 'You must never ever bring them indoors.'

'Didn't you know?' said Miss Ada who adds the more kindly note to a reprimand. 'They carry misfortune.'

Bad luck in flowers?'

'Exceedingly,' Miss Lily nodded. 'Always brings in a death. Or some other malhappence.'

'Like the night Lily was born,' said Miss Ada, 'Mother says she brought thorn flowers in.' Miss Lily gave a knife-edged look.

I said how sorry I was. But I wasn't really. I don't see how a flowery twig can possibly bring anything into a house except a nicer smell than the one that's there already. 'Are they supposed to be poisonous or something?'

But they'd begun arguing over whether in fact I had picked the one that Mother Hoggin wouldn't allow indoors, or was it one of the others? Blackthorn, or whitethorn, or maythorn?

Miss Ada decided on whitethorn because it carries with it, not bad, but good fortune.

'You must remember, Lily, Mother telling us how the whitethorn will cure the milk-fever in a cow and skin-warts in a child?'

If I'd had some warts, I'd have asked her how it was done.

'Don't contradict me, Ada. You know I remember everything important better than ever you did. Blackthorn, that is what the girl brought in. You saw it. It's name is black and so is its nature and it flowers well before Ash Wednesday. The mayflower is pink and flowers in May, in time for Ascension Day. I don't know anything about your whitethorn.'

So much silliness over a name. You'd think by their ages they'd have given up arguing.

I said, 'Why don't you look it up in a book?'

'Hagathorn!' exclaimed Miss Ada triumphantly. 'Mother said it was the hagathorn we must not bring in.'

In like a lion

Yesterday the earth tipped further toward the sun without me noticing the jolt. It was almost like summer. Fluffy clouds like sheep danced across a high blue sky. The bare trees all glowed. The lichen on their trunks makes them gold.

Before tea, I watched the sun go down behind the bare trees. There was a streak of purple cloud across it. Purple is the colour people used to wear for funerals, before they thought of black. If you stare back at the sun for long enough, it makes your eyes go dazzly.

In the night, wild winds came screaming in out of nowhere. We were woken by the noise, like Mr Hoggin stamping on the tin roof, kicking at the walls, rampaging. Bang, shudder, creak. Smaller winds slapped against the windows like the big palm of his hand. Slap, slap, slap. I lay and listened.

'Pity the poor sailor on such a night as this,' Mother Hoggin used to say. I pitied him. The wind outside makes you think of being on a boat tossing on the waves. It makes you shiver even though you're tucked up safe in bed.

Above the roar, I heard crying, like Mrs Tiggywinkle. She hates the wind in her ears. It makes them twitch. She goes all anxious. She shouldn't be out there. She should be curled up in her cardboard box by Miss Lily's fire.

I got up and looked out into the lashing dark. Rain was coming down with such force that it bounced off the ground as though it was raining upwards as well as downwards and sideways. I opened the window to call for Mrs Tiggywinkle. The wind grabbed hold of the frame with such force that it practically broke my arm getting it shut again.

'Hannah! What on earth are you up to now?' Esther said.

'Looking for Mrs Tiggy,' I said.

'Oh for goodness sake!' Esther said. She pulled her pillow over her head.

In the morning we discovered the wind had done something horrible and devastating to Miss Ada and Miss Lily's home. Such is the power of nature.

I wondered if it was my fault. If I'd made it happen by bringing in bad luck flowers.

ELEVEN

Where the winds blow

Windy change

When Esther plugged in the kettle, there was a blue zig-zag across the kitchen. The lights went out and the radio went off just as the forecaster was warning us about the gales.

'Now that's what they call a truly electric personality,' I said with a giggle.

But Esther didn't think it was at all funny. 'Don't you realise I might have been killed!' she said.

'Bother!' said Mum. 'Wretched trip switch gone again.'

She went and checked beside the fuse-box in the passage. But it wasn't that.

'Electric's right off. Must be a line come down somewhere.'

So it was pure coincidence. Esther hasn't got an electric persona after all.

We had to go without tea for our breakfast. So did Dad. Mum usually takes him through a cup before she leaves for work. She says it's to make his empty day start kindly.

We were just setting off when Mum said, 'Oh heavens, Hannah. What about your old ladies?'

So they're mine now, are they?

'If ours is off, their's will be too.'

'They'll be all right.'

'How will they manage?'

I said, 'They've got the fire. They don't use electricity. Miss Lily says it's too dangerous for Miss Ada. She burned out their kettle.'

Outside, the wind was frothing everything up like egg-beaters. Leaves and twigs and fir-cones and gobbets of mud. Two beech trees had blown over. Their roots were sticking up sideways in the air and a chunky old oak had cracked in half like a hollow tooth. It was like a bridge across the lane. One of its branches had fallen into Miss Ada and Miss Lily's roof. The chimney stack and a bit of wall were crumbled up like a smashed sandcastle.

I went over. Mum followed.

The first person I met was Mrs Tiggywinkle, cowering sneakily under a holly bush. She skipped out to meet me, all pussy smiles, as though I was suddenly her favourite person, as though she'd never in her life even considered desertion.

Inside, they'd taken up normal positions, Miss Lily, to the left of the fire-place, or what would have been the fire-place if it were still there, and Miss Ada against the table spreading bread. Mrs Tiggywinkle came in with me, cautiously sniffed the dusty confusion and went out. The kitchen was even colder than usual so they were wearing blankets and raincoats over their jersey layers. Miss Ada had her nylon overall tightly over the top of everything else so she looked strangely fat. There was no fire in the grate because of there being no grate, no hearth.

But even with a hole upstairs in the roof, and with the whole of their chimney-stack which had come tumbling down the flue spilling out into the room like a volcanic lava flow of bricks and soot and bits of burned feathers and bird's nests, we had to go through the ritual.

'Good morning, Miss Lily.'

'Good morning, Hannah.'

'Good morning Miss Ada.'

'Oh!' Her startled surprise to see me in the doorway. 'So it's you today, is it?'

'Say good morning to her, Ada,' said Miss Lily.

'Good morning, Hannah dear. And what have you brought us today?'

'Nothing. May I come in?'

Miss Lily said, 'If you wish. Don't outstay your welcome. Ada has a lot to do today.'

There's a film of soot and mortar dust over everything, including the bread and margarine, and over Miss Lily, and instead of being on the footstool in front of her, her stumpy dusty feet are propped up on the pile of rubble. Where is her stool? Perhaps it's buried.

'I think,' says Mum slowly. 'I'd better go and get my husband to see what he can do to help.'

'Thank you kindly,' says Miss Lily, daintily sipping cold sooty water from her tea-cup. 'But that won't be necessary. My sister manages perfectly well for the both of us.'

Miss Ada nods. 'Yes, yes, yes. The geese are fed. Isn't that right? So we'll go into the parlour till it's over.'

Miss Lily says, 'Ada! You're talking smoke and gammon. We'll get on as we always have.'

'That's right, Lily. We'll sit tight till Mother comes home. She'll know what to do.'

Mum signals something silently to me and rolls her eyes like a goldfish. 'I think they're probably in shock,' she mouths.

They seem pretty normal to me.

At first, Dad was grumpy about being hauled out of bed without even the comfort of a cuppa. But once he discovered he could be Chief Co-Ordinator of Rescue Services, he perked up and began striding about and talking in a loud voice and waving his arms about. Mum left him to it and went off to work.

Within a couple of hours, Dad had got Pegg Bottom seething with vehicles. There must have been more outsiders crammed into our hamlet than it's seen for decades.

The chain-saw men sliced up the fallen trees. A line of Dad's drinking pals from *The Harrow* passed rubble out of the cottage hand to hand. A police car arrived with its blue light flashing to warn the hedges and trees, owls and foxes, that help was at hand. Then a doctor arrived who made Miss Lily very upset. She protested that as she hadn't called him out she wasn't going to waste her money paying him.

'Not so much as a farthing of mine will he get,' she said. 'And don't you go badgering my poor sister for it either.'

An ambulance came most of the way down the lane but was turned back because the doctor decided a health visitor and a social worker would be more useful. The victims were in such splendid health but refusing to budge.

Dad suddenly noticed I was still hanging around his site of special emergency interest.

'I say, Esther, shouldn't you be off at school by now? Your sister left hours ago.'

'I'm not Esther,' I said. 'I'm the other one. And we've got the morning off.' It wasn't really lying because once I'd said it, I sort of believed it. And more importantly, so did he.

'Your sister never mentioned it.'

'Just my class. Staff training or something.'

So Dad got me handing out cups of watery orange squash to those who looked as though they needed it.

Although it was the right thing that Miss Lily and Miss Ada were being rescued by all these busy people, Pegg Bottom didn't feel half so private and special as when there was no-one else here except grumpy Broddys and stoical Hoggins.

By midday the people from the electricity board had fixed the power back on. The rubble had gone onto a new pile outside by the old tip. There was still a hole in the roof. But Dad and his trusty mates, fortified by orange squash, began fixing a green tarpaulin over it.

The doctor and the health visitor left. A social worker came. She was a bit scruffy. She said her name was Miss Pardon and she had a badge in her bag to prove it. I wonder if she's related to Mrs Pardon.

She told Miss Lily and Miss Ada that the doctor, the health visitor and she, had all come to the decision that they ought to be moved. Personally, I thought they ought to have been asked first.

Miss Lily pursed up her lips. 'Just as soon as my sister can get the kettle to boil, I'll be having my tea.'

'It's really in your very best interests,' said Miss Pardon with an encouraging smile that showed she had a front tooth missing just like her ancestor. The place she had in mind was The Old Hall. 'Just up the road. I could take you there rightaway. You've nothing to lose by taking a look round.'

'What about our poor pussy cat?' said Miss Ada.

'We can be back within the hour. Though if you do decide to move, I'm sure my department can find a friendly neighbour to take it in.'

'And the livestock? Who'll feed the hens and the geese?'

'Pull yourself together, Ada,' said Miss Lily sternly. 'You know Mother sold the geese long ago. Come along. We'd better go with this woman and have done with it. Just so long as you don't expect us to accept if it doesn't meet with our approval.'

Once Miss Lily agreed, Miss Ada did. I tagged along with them. Miss Pardon didn't seem to mind.

'Of course you can come too. It's always reassuring for people to have a familiar face.'

Miss Ada said, 'But we don't know who she is.'

'Of course we do,' snapped Miss Lily. 'The girl's our maid.

We've always kept an indoor servant. We've always lived very pleasantly.'

Up at the Old Hall

Miss Pardon must have been used to moving stubborn old people about. She got Miss Lily into the front passenger seat of her car with almost no trouble at all. I sat in the back with Miss Ada. Neither of them had a clue about seat belts. I had to do up Miss Ada's for her.

Miss Pardon said, 'It's a wonder nobody's ever thought to offer you a Zimmer frame. It could make all the difference to your quality of life.'

'My sister and I have always managed quite satisfactorily,' Miss Lily replied. I don't think she had a clue what a Zimmer frame was.

'To help with your mobility. A walking frame,' said Miss Pardon.

'My sister does all the walking that's necessary for us, thank you.'

Now that the Hall is an old folks' home, I don't think it's as grand as it used to be. There's a sign at the gate which says, *The Old Hall, Rest Home for the Elderly & Infirm. CSM registered. NCHA approved.* But the paint's all peeling.

As we drove along the overgrown avenue, I tried to imagine what it must have looked like when Dora walked up here on her first day. I wondered if she'd felt nervous about coming to such a big place. I wondered if she'd married Mr Hoggin just to get away from being a maid. I was really expecting Miss

Lily and Miss Ada to do the melting. But they were both very quiet as though their power lines had been switched off.

'I am warden of the Old Hall,' said the woman waiting to greet Miss Ada at the top of the front steps.

Prisons have wardens.

Miss Lily wouldn't get out of the car, even when two people in blue nurse's uniforms came running down the steps to assist Miss Pardon.

'You won't be able to see the lovely rose garden, or the fish pond,' they pleaded.

'There's no need for a fuss. I can see what I need from here. And I believe I can trust my sister on all other matters. So there'll be no incidents, will there, Ada?'

Miss Ada shook her head. Wibble-wobble goes the bobble.

Miss Lily folded her hands across her lap as though locking a five-barred gate. All she can see is a red-brick wall in front of where Miss Pardon's parked.

I went with Miss Ada. She seemed to be shrinking inside her layers of jersies till only a knitted pom-pom and a little wizened faze peeped out at the top.

The entrance hall to the Old Hall is mega. There's a great fire-place on one side. But it wasn't lit. There was an old pickle jar in the grate instead, filled with dried grass and flowers. They'd lost their colour. Dried flowers always do. Katy's mother used to do dry flower arrangements. The dust settles on them. They go grey and papery. I hate dried flowers.

The Warden said, 'We keep the place as homely as we can,' as she held open the gates of the lift. 'It's this way, Ada. Up on the third floor.' She didn't even call her Miss Ada.

Miss Ada looked at the lift. It might have been an electric chair waiting for her, if she'd known what an electric chair was.

'I have never,' she began. I think she wanted to say that she'd never been in a lift before. 'I'm not so sure I can do this.'

'Come along now, Ada.' The warden seized Miss Ada round the waist and hoisted her in before she could resist.

'That's right,' said Miss Ada. The gates clanged shut. 'My sister said, No incidents.' She peered out like a mouse trapped in a cage as she and the Warden went clanking upwards. There was only room for two. Miss Pardon and I had to use the stairs. I wanted to arrive at the same time as Miss Ada. So I ran. The staircase wound round the lift shaft. Four sides of a square for every floor. I thought my lungs would burst.

The room in the attic was poky with a slanting skylight. If you hadn't got cataracts and if you happened to be as tall as a giraffe with the lookout instincts of a meercat, you might have got a glimpse of the tops of some trees. Miss Ada couldn't. It was the sort of room a servant would have slept in and I don't expect they were meant to waste time craning their necks to admire the view. There were two narrow iron beds crammed in.

'Share?' said Miss Ada. 'Like young girls again?'

'A home from home for the elderly confused is what we offer, *par excellence*,' the Warden said. 'Care with dignity is our belief. As you can understand, there's heavy demand for places. But, providing there are no outstanding medical problems – ?'

Miss Pardon shook her head. 'None at all, apart from some short-term memory loss.'

The Warden kept on explaining to Miss Pardon what a wonderful place it was, as though it was she, not Miss Ada, who had to decide if she and her sister wanted to stay. 'There's a television aerial point in every room. So of course you may bring your own set and a few of your own treasures if you wish. As you see, we've modernised completely. Wash basin, power point. Fitted carpets.'

It didn't take long to inspect. So we all came down again.

I wanted to tell Miss Ada, Don't do it. Say no. Don't accept retirement from life. Go back home where you belong. Bolt the door and stay there. Never fly in an electric cage again. Up fifteen twisty steps is the proper way to reach your bed.

I looked into one of the downstairs lounges. In the days when Dora dusted the cornices and swept out the grate it must have been very grand.

More dried flowers in the grate now. And the room lined with the living dead. Propped up in their armchairs to look as though they were sleeping. The windows were sealed. It was hot and stuffy.

'And we have lots of activities. Memory Club. Extend. Creative therapies. Our Down-Forget-Me-Not Lane afternoons are lots of fun. So you'll be letting us know your decision within twenty-four hours? We can't hold the room longer than that.'

Back in Miss Pardon's car, Miss Ada said, 'It's perfectly adequate, Lily. We'll be quite content there.' If she'd been anybody else you might have thought she was crying.

Ascension day

Miss Lily was cunning and cruel. She knew she wasn't going to be shoved into a servant's attic room. In the night she found a way out of it.

She died, still sitting upright in her chair. She left Miss Ada behind to cope all by herself. Mrs Tiggywinkle returned of her own accord to live with me.

With nobody to tell her what to do, Miss Ada shrunk down to the size of a tiny desiccated chrysalis. She put her head on one side like a child appealing for approval.

'Did I do right?' she asks me, squeezing my hand in hers which is slippery with margarine. 'I didn't think I should light the fire this morning, not with her sitting so close or her boots might have scorched.'

What is Miss Ada going to do with the rest of her life if she doesn't have sliced bread to spread?

Inside me, I already knew that Miss Ada wouldn't be doing any more melting.

TWELVE

When history ends

No more weather. It's practically summer.

I was really glad to be in school for the lesson when Mrs Gribbon gave us back our project work. Now that Miss Lily has died, my *History of the Hoggins* is even more important.

I was so eager to hear what she'd thought of it that I actually moved forward to an empty desk near the front. More fool me. I should've realised long ago that I'm the no-hope, dope-head of the class as far as she's concerned.

'Ah, Hannah,' said Mrs Gribbon. 'Nice to have you back.'

What's she on about?

'Now. One or two people have unfortunately produced some very inappropriate work,' she began.

It didn't occur to me that I might be one of them. 'For example, those who decided to add artistic decorative elements to their work.'

That wasn't me. That had to be Mandy. Roses and silly rabbits in hats.

Mrs Gribbon made no mentions, oblique or otherwise,

about my magnificent effort. Instead, she asked me to wait behind to speak to her after the lesson. So of course I did. I was still feeling buoyant. Obviously she hadn't wanted to show special favours to me in front of the rest of them so she was going to congratulate me now.

'Hannah,' she said, then stopped for a long pause as though she'd forgotten what she wanted to say. She breathed in and out a few times and began again. 'Hannah. I hardly know what to say. Copious, definitely. Voluminous? Yes. Hours of time must have gone into producing all er, this er–.'

'This *History of the Hoggins*, Miss,' I said, to help her out in case she'd forgotten the title. 'It's meant to be a sort of tribute to them.'

'D'you know, Hannah, I thought you must have handed in the wrong work to the wrong teacher. I even went and had a word with Mr McCluskie about it.'

How could it be the wrong homework?

'You haven't done what you were asked to do.'

'Yes I did! The only thing different is I already knew them. So I didn't need to interview them like you said.'

One of the annoying things about teachers is that, when one small part of something is wrong, they decide they won't accept any of it.

'These are fairy-tales, I have to admit they are unusual and charming. But I do not teach your creative writing course. I teach history, the continuous, methodical, systematic and critical recording of past events. From the Greek word, *historia*. Which means?'

I shrugged. 'How should I know?' She was supposed to be the teacher who knew things.

'You have obviously forgotten we discussed it in the class. Or perhaps you were off in one of your funny little day-dreams. Or perhaps it was even one of the days you failed to turn up at all. *Historia* means finding out, by enquiry. It does not mean making up out of your head. You see Hannah, if you want to do well, and I'm sure you have it in you, if you want to be allowed to sit for the examinations with some likelihood of passing, you are going to have to stay awake, to listen, to complete your homework, not just when you happen to be feeling inspired. It doesn't matter how poetic you are on the page if it's the wrong subject.'

I was gob-smacked that she didn't like it.

'It's the right subject. It's all true what I wrote.'

'Two centenarians living alone in a hut in the woods.'

'It wasn't a hut. It was a very old dwelling. And they were the living history like you wanted. So old they were like sort of ghosts.'

Mrs Gribbon kept sighing and shaking her head. 'Ghosts, Hannah, is not what you were asked to investigate. And as for all this strange stuff about people melting into each other.'

She was deliberately mis-reading it, trying to make out that Miss Violet and Miss Rose had never even existed.

'They couldn't possibly melt into *each other*. That would be stupid. They went back to *themselves*, as they were, not to someone different.'

She handed me back the bundle of notebooks and loose

pages. They were in much more of a muddle than when I first put them on her desk. She didn't say sorry. But at least, having slagged me off for ten minutes, she now softened up.

'I really do want to help you. I know that you and your family have been having a tough time of it.'

Was she going to say something awful about Dad?

'But it's not the end of the world when a parent is made redundant. Round here, families have long since grown used to unemployment. It's nothing to be ashamed of. And it should give you all the more incentive to do well to make your parents happy. So I thought if I gave you, as a special exception, an extension, say till next week, you'd have a breathing space to get this together properly.'

It was break-time. I could see other people from my class lying about on the newly-mown grass outside while I was stuck here in the classroom. I stared out of the window very hard, trying to make my eyes go buzzy. I do not want to be here. I want to be somewhere else, anywhere else. I want to be going fishing with Humphrey.

'So till next week then? And don't forget, we need facts, dear, not fancies.'

How can I give her facts. There weren't enough to fill half a page.

Two females lived in the same place, sat by the same fire, saw the same trees out of the same windows, every single day for a lifetime. They didn't marry, didn't fight wars, didn't vote, never went anywhere.

And now one of them is dead.

The buzzer went for the end of break. The rest of my class were getting ready for P.E. I'm not bothered with P.E. I decided to go and visit Miss Ada.

No brooches

In June, dog-roses are flowering in the hedgerows. From a distance, they look like a mass of white butterflies fluttering all over the hedge. But close to, I could see the petals, very pale pink like a newborn baby's cheeks. In the middle, there's a fluff of golden yellow like a red-haired baby's carrotty curls.

I know roses don't carry bad luck, only thorns which can be pulled off the stems. So I carefully picked some, and dethorned them.

They're sitting in their armchairs in the circle of lifeless relics, staring ahead. One of the others shows a sign of movement, turns her head and smiles as I stand in the doorway trying to work out which one is Miss Ada.

'Visitor for you, Ada!' calls the attendant. They still don't know to call her 'Miss Ada'.

She doesn't wear a brown velvet bow in her hair any more. They've cut it short and given it a curly perm so she looks just like all the other ladies. It's mostly ladies. They've given her a pair of glasses too. And whoever dresses her, doesn't fasten her cardigan front with the five different brooches she used to like to wear. Perhaps they don't know what she likes because they haven't asked her.

She looks at me when I show her the dog-roses. But she doesn't take them so I lay them in her lap.

'Ada, Ada!' shouts the attendant in her ear, shaking her shoulder. 'Look, it's your little friend from down the road! Popped in to see you. Brought you flowers, isn't that nice?'

She says, 'Thank you,' but she doesn't recognise me.

She isn't happy. She isn't unhappy. I don't think I want to visit her any more.

Riding away down the long drive, I heard noises all round me. I know it's only the breeze in the top branches of the trees. But I still wish I wasn't on my own. I pedalled extra fast until I saw a man plodding up the driveway, with his head down. I couldn't see him clearly because the shadows of the trees were dancing across his face. But I knew it was Mr Hoggin.

I was scared. When he's drunk he can be so angry. I tried to calm myself. After all, he's not really there. I got off my bike and stood still as a fence under a tree. Then he won't see me. I'm not here. I'm invisible.

He saw. And he knew who I was.

'Evening miss,' he growled and tipped his cap at me, civil but not friendly. He was not drunk.

'Good evening Mr Hoggin,' I said. It came out as a frightened squeak.

'You won't have heard then.'

'Heard?'

'The missus is in a bad way. We lost the lad. Humphrey.'

'Lost him?'

'We got the telegram from his unit. Died of his wounds.' Then he shuffled on. He'd had the final disappointment of his life. I'd heard people say that he went into the woods and hanged himself. It isn't true. I know he died of natural causes.

I was crying when I reached home. Esther must have warned Mum I'd got a Detention for bunking off too much. Of course it wasn't that. I got sad about things but I'd never get upset about school.

It was Humphrey. Stupid to be sad when I'd always known that he was going to be killed in France. He was only sixteen. And now his pink cheeks gone for ever and he was never to know how much I felt for him.

Misdummer madness

After that, everything went from wrong to worse. It's all Mrs Gribbon's fault. Or perhaps it was mine. I should never have let her see my notebooks and I should certainly never have tried to explain it to her. It got her worried and it made her start interfering.

She went and told some of the other teachers. It seems my form teacher knew all about Dad and why we moved here, and they decided I'd better see someone called Ed Syke. I heard them say it several times. I really did think that was his name. Actually, they said Ed. Psych., which means Educational Psychologist. He's the doc. who copes with loopy boys and girls who see things that aren't there, and hears things that aren't being said.

All because of Mrs Nosy-Parker Gribbon, I was being referred to the nuthead man.

Naturally, I didn't want to go. 'I'm *not* mad, Mum,' I said.

'Really I'm not. Don't let them say I'm mad. I'm a lot saner than Dad was all winter.'

'But, Hannah, please listen darling,' said Mum. 'It's not just about your ghosts. It's also because of the not-going-to-school when you should have been.'

It seems I've been bunking off quite a lot. I was quite surprised. I hadn't really noticed.

I asked Esther if it was true.

She said, 'Er, yes actually Han.'

'Where did I go? What did I do all day?'

'You used to roam about in the woods, I think. Sit under dead trees eating your sandwiches. Hang about outside the old cottage.'

They don't call it truanting, not like they did when Humphrey was young. They call it being a disaffected school refuser, which is daft. I don't remember refusing to do anything.

It seems that if you're one of these refusers, your parents get the blame. They can even be sent to jail for it. More usually, they're fined. Mrs Gribbon must have realised that on Mum's *Contented Turkey* wages it would take about a hundred years to pay off a fine so she'd end up having to go to jail. Or Dad would.

Luckily, it hasn't come to that. Instead, I served time on Thursdays sitting in a bleak, bare office with frosted windows and a glaring overhead strip light. I didn't have to do hard labour. I just had to talk.

I never did find out if Ed Syke has a real name. At least it

146

got me off doing Physical Education. I hate competitive team sports. I told him so.

I said, 'And I reckon with all that biking I have to do to get anywhere away from Pegg Bottom, I don't need netball and rounders as well.'

He said, 'So would you call yourself a bit of a loner, Hannah?'

'No,' I said. 'Not specially.'

'But you're not much of a joiner-in, are you?' He had obviously decided already what he thought I was, so there was no point arguing.

In the end, after loads more Thursday sessions, he forced me to agree that I hadn't really seen Ada and Lily when they were young, nor Humphrey, nor Mr and Mrs Hoggin and all the little Hoggins.

'Though I could have seen their ghosts, couldn't I?' I said. 'The imprints they made on time, even if I didn't actually see them?'

No. According to Ed, they are all figments of my imagination. Or wish fulfilment. Wishing I wasn't where I was, but was somewhere else, like the past, because that was more manageable since one knew the outcome.

He's got it all sussed. According to him, I've been having some kind of breakdown with delusions, all caused by the difficulty of the move and Dad's depression. I don't believe it. Lots of people have to move house. Lots of people's dad's have troubles and get depressed. Some people don't even have dads.

The Ed. Syke saw Mum and Dad too, and Esther. All separately.

I wish Mrs Tiggywinkle could speak. She knows. *She'd* tell him what was going on.

I was going to say to him, 'Why don't you interview my cat next? She *knows* it happened.' But then I realised that if I ever mention a word about speaking cats, he'll decide I'm seriously off my trolley.

So I'm going along with his theory of emotional upset and instability. It'll cause less hassle for Mum.

September 29th

How come we're come back here again? Where did the year disappear to? How did it pass so quickly?

The Misses Hoggins used to call this Michaelmas, like the tall blue daisies that grow round the compost heap.

The days and the trees are golden. Other people call this the Indian summer, so Mum says.

'It's like a reprieve before winter returns.'

Will all the seasons, for the rest of my life, go dashing by like this, each one dispersing before I've had time to grab hold of it? Will I find myself suddenly, an old woman, Ms Hannah, with my even older sister, Ms Esther?

Will we still be living together in some old folks' centre, squabbling over who's taking up more room at the card table?

Esther crashes into our room and nudges me in the ribs.

'Come on Han! Stop day-dreaming.'

'I'm not. I'm writing up my journal.'

'Finish it tomorrow. We'll be late if you don't get a move on.'

It's Family Disco and Harvest Barbecue at school. We're all going. (Except for Mrs Tiggywinkle. She'll stay and guard the home.) The four of us. Mum and Dad. Yes, Dad too. He's on the P.T.A. committee this term. On our bikes. They've both got bikes now so we're a mobile, eight-wheel family. Dad's outside checking all the tyres.

Another extraordinary thing. Dad's starting school next Monday! At his age!

They run adult classes in the evenings. Computer studies, cake decorating. Car maintenance. He's applied to do the carpentry course and train to be a furniture-maker.

'A real craftsman,' says Mum proudly.

And the first thing he's going to make is a roll-top desk for me, with lockable drawers.

'So you can sit and write your secrets in comfort,' he says, giving me a hug. 'When you're not doing your homework like a good girl.'

'What about Ess?'

It seems Esther doesn't want anything more than to make sure we all get to the disco on time so she can goggle over her latest dream man. If only she had Mrs Pardon's magic charm for love.

She hands me my hair-brush as a hint to get a move on. She says, 'And d'you want to borrow my busty bandeau? Just for tonight?'

It's new, skinny-rib, all glittery. I say, Yes. She lets me use some of her new body spray too. It's called *Phantôme de L'Esprit*. That means Ghost of the Spirit.

Dad's ringing his bike bell to signal he's ready.

'Come on girls!' Mum calls.

Off we go. Family fun. I know I'm dead lucky to have this family.

WATERBOUND

Jane Stemp

The City is a place of rules, a place where Admin is always watching . . . a place where there is no room to be different.

Under the City, the river flows from light into dark, into an unknown place. A place which hides a secret. Something forbidden – out of sight and out of mind.

There Gem finds the Waterbound, the children the City forgot. She joins in their fight to be part of the world she knows.

Why are they underground? Is there a way out?

HAUNTINGS

Susan Price

'Why?' I said. 'Why does she come back?'
Gran said: 'Why was her murdered, poor
wench?'
Take it from me, that's what they're like, real
hauntings. All it takes to bring you to your
knees in suffocating fear is the sound of
walking and the jingle of a bunch of keys.

Ten terrifying hauntings that will linger
in your mind long after, that will make
you glance over your shoulder, that will
fill you with delicious unease . . . These
are some of the best ghost stories you will
ever read.

A truly outstanding collection by a master
storyteller and winner of the *Carnegie
Medal*.

THE FATED SKY

Henrietta Branford

There was a dragon in the sky the night before the stranger came. It flamed across the red west from the cliffs to the black road of the sea. It did not speak to me. But I feared it.

After the death of her father and brothers in a viking raid, Ran is alone. Alone and afraid. Travelling by sledge across a snowy headland to take part in the winter sacrifice, her future is uncertain.

Her fate lies in the hands of Vigut, a cruel stranger who brings nothing but fear and death. Her life at the mercy of an evil magician. Her destiny in the love of a travelling musician. But where the journey ends is up to her . . .

ORDER FORM